Greek Island Brides

Finding love that lasts to infinity!

All marriages that take place on renowned wedding destination Infinity Island are guaranteed to last forever!

And the picturesque Greek island is about to weave its magic for friends Lea, Popi and Stasia. They dream of finding their own happy-ever-afters... And they're about to meet three billionaires who will sweep them off their feet—and down the aisle!

Follow Lea's journey from surprise pregnancy to dream proposal in

Carrying the Greek Tycoon's Baby

Available now!

And look out for Popi's and Stasia's stories

Coming soon!

Dear Reader,

Sometimes you have to leave what you've always known and set off on an adventure to truly learn what you're capable of. And sometimes when the odds seem against you and you persevere it works out better than you could have ever imagined.

This is what happens when Lea Romes finds out that she's inherited a wedding island in the Mediterranean. Not even knowing that she had family in Greece, she is eager to find out more about her ancestors. But when a tall, sexy man crosses her path, there's a chance for an island romance.

Xander Marinakos is a real estate tycoon. And he's intent on buying Infinity Island, but there's one thing standing in his way: Lea. There's something about her that has this workaholic thinking of everything but work. And when his business offer is firmly rebuffed, things take a much more personal turn.

A few months later, Xander has vowed to put the memories of the beauty with the greenish-blue eyes behind him and absorb himself in work. Until a phone call changes everything. He's about to become a daddy.

Thank you for joining Xander and Lea as they are reunited on the sunny Greek island where romance is in the air. Their lives are about to change in ways they never imagined.

Happy reading,

Jennifer

Carrying the Greek Tycoon's Baby

———

Jennifer Faye

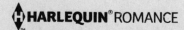
HARLEQUIN®ROMANCE

Recycling programs
for this product may
not exist in your area.

ISBN-13: 978-1-335-49926-4

Carrying the Greek Tycoon's Baby

First North American publication 2019

Copyright © 2019 by Jennifer F. Stroka

Printed in U.S.A.

Award-winning author **Jennifer Faye** pens fun, heartwarming contemporary romances with rugged cowboys, sexy billionaires and enchanting royalty. Internationally published, with books translated into nine languages, she is a two-time winner of the *RT Book Reviews* Reviewers' Choice Award. She has also won the CataRomance Reviewers' Choice Award, been named a Top Pick author and been nominated for numerous other awards.

Books by Jennifer Faye

Harlequin Romance

The Cattaneos' Christmas Miracles

Heiress's Royal Baby Bombshell

Once Upon a Fairytale

Beauty and Her Boss
Miss White and the Seventh Heir

Mirraccino Marriages

The Millionaire's Royal Rescue
Married for His Secret Heir

Brides for the Greek Tycoons

The Greek's Ready-Made Wife
The Greek's Nine-Month Surprise

Her Festive Baby Bombshell
Snowbound with an Heiress

Visit the Author Profile page
at Harlequin.com for more titles.

PROLOGUE

March, Infinity Island, Greece

THINGS WOULD GET better.

They had to.

Lea Romes refused to accept any other alternative.

She pushed her chair back from the desk with its insurmountable pile of paperwork. In this modern age of technology, she thought paperwork would be a thing of the past. But alas, it seemed as though dealing with written documents would be a constant while the digital correspondence and spreadsheets just added to the burden.

At least she got to work in paradise as a wedding planner. She picked up her oversized coffee mug and moved to the French doors overlooking the private cove. She stepped out onto the spacious balcony, letting the vibrant sun warm her face. Since she'd inherited the island some thirteen months ago, her life had changed dramatically.

Her move from Seattle, Washington, to Greece had happened not in a matter of months or even weeks but days. Of course, it hadn't helped that she'd learned she had extended family in Greece from an attorney instead of her own parents—

parents who had deprived her of that part of her life. It was a betrayal she'd never seen coming. She'd felt utterly blindsided and hurt beyond belief.

With nothing more than two suitcases and a disillusioned view of life, she'd set out on her journey to Greece. She hadn't known what to expect when she arrived on this small, lush Greek island. The attorney had informed her that Infinity Island had been in the family for generations. It wasn't until she browsed through all of the photos in the family home that she realized her own mother had been born and raised on this very island. It was like an arrow to the heart. How could her mother have kept this place and her family from her?

Lea hadn't spoken to her parents since their heated argument right before she left Seattle. But it wasn't like they'd reached out to her, either. Her parents were stubborn and so certain they'd done the right thing by omitting certain details of Lea's life. But right now Lea had bigger problems, starting with the fact that this wedding/honeymoon destination spot was in deep financial trouble—

Knock. Knock.

Lea stepped back inside the office. "Come in."

Popi Costas, her best friend and the other wedding planner on the island, stuck her head inside the office. Her dark brown ponytail swung over her shoulder. "Your guest has arrived."

"Already?" That couldn't be right. He wasn't due to arrive for another hour. Her gaze sought out the little smiling emoji clock on her desk. It was in fact 10 a.m. Not 9 a.m. Time had gotten away from her.

She'd wanted to touch up her makeup and hair before greeting this man—this very important man. She'd seen his photos on the internet. He was strikingly handsome in that tall, dark and mysterious sort of way. But she assured herself that wanting to fix herself up and put on a good—no, a great—first impression had more to do with business than anything else. He might just be the person to change everything for her and this island.

"Quit frowning," Popi said. They'd become fast friends when Lea had arrived on the island. It helped that they were of similar age and Popi was easy to be around. She could make Lea smile, even when she didn't want to. "You look amazing. As always." Popi gestured with her hand. "Come on. You don't want to keep him waiting."

She was right. The last thing Lea wanted to do was give this man a bad impression right from the start. She dashed out the door, wishing she'd taken more time that morning in front of the mirror. She sighed. There wasn't time to do anything about it now.

Outside, the sun was shining brightly in the clear blue sky. One thing about living on a Greek island versus Seattle was there was sunshine almost every day of the year. And Lea loved it. Arriving on Infinity Island had felt, strangely enough, like coming home.

She climbed on the golf cart that she used to get around the small island. They had a whole fleet of golf carts for their guests as well as paved paths. She quickly maneuvered her way down to the marina. Most of their guests arrived from the mainland via a ferry or flew in via a chartered seaplane. In rare cases, a helicopter was used—but generally that was saved for emergencies or the occasional guest who could afford such extravagances.

When she'd first arrived on the island, she'd spent all her spare moments of that first month venturing down every meandering path littered with wild flowers and blazing some paths of her own. She'd met every human and every goat, of which there were many, that resided on the island. Most people there worked for the wedding business in one manner or another. They were like one big family and they'd welcomed her with open arms. Lea couldn't imagine a friendlier place.

Just then she noticed a seaplane preparing to take off over the calm blue sea. But it was the man in the dark suit standing on the wooden dock, with his back to her, that caught her attention. She took in his immense height and broad, muscled shoulders accentuated by his suit jacket—a very fine set of threads. It probably cost more than she made in a month. Definitely.

His dark hair was trimmed in a short neat cut just like in his online photos. Not a strand was out of place. She wondered if he liked his life to be just as neat and orderly. As she continued to stare, she imagined what it'd be like to comb her fingertips through his hair. Her fingers tingled with temptation. She tightened her hold on the steering wheel.

Lea tramped the brakes, causing the cart to skid to a halt. She quickly alighted and moved across the dock toward the man. His attire continued to draw her curiosity. Did he not realize he was coming to an island? Around here swim trunks were more common than a suit jacket. When the man turned to her, she realized he was also wearing a tie. She inwardly groaned. If he was as uptight as his appearance, she was in big trouble.

As the departing plane flew overhead, she leveled her shoulders and stepped forward. She held out her hand. "Hello. I'm Lea Romes."

The man's dark brows rose in surprise. "You are in charge?"

When she nodded, he took her hand in his. His grip was firm. She could tell just from his touch that he was quite strong. So, there was more to this man than just a designer suit.

Her gaze rose to his clean-shaven jaw and his mouth that was pressed into a firm line, not giving away what he was thinking. She'd caught him off guard at first but he seemed to have regained his composure.

When her gaze met his, she couldn't read anything in his dark eyes. So she decided to smile, hoping to lighten the mood. "Welcome to Infinity Island."

"Do you have many guests?" He withdrew his hand and glanced around at the quiet morning.

So much for the pleasantries.

She schooled her expression so as not to frown at his obvious lack of social niceties. "Not at the moment. We're expecting guests to begin arriving tomorrow for an upcoming wedding."

"So right now, the island is deserted, other than staff?"

She shook her head. "Not exactly. We have some honeymooners as well as some couples who have returned for a renewal of their vows and a second honeymoon."

He frowned. Apparently that was the wrong answer.

"If you'd like to come this way—" she gestured toward the golf cart "—I can give you the grand tour."

"Is there much to see?"

Was he being serious? Or was he being sarcastic? It was impossible for her to tell as neither his tone nor his expression changed much. His gaze continued to scan the area. And so she did the same, trying to see Infinity through his eyes. There was lots of green foliage interspersed with red, yellow, pink, purple and blue blooms. Wild orchids grew everywhere. A few of the buildings overlooked the cove. Her office happened to be one of them. And then she realized the problem.

She swallowed hard and turned to him. "You can't see much of the resort from here as the island has been strategically planned. The buildings have been placed in various locations over the island instead of concentrated in one spot." She should have grabbed a map of the island for him. It was something that was distributed to all the guests with their welcome basket. "Trust me. There's a lot to the island including acres of vegetable gardens. We grow most of our own food."

His gaze met hers, but she couldn't read his thoughts. "Let's proceed."

He bent over and it was only then that she noticed he had an overnight bag. She hadn't expected him to want to stay. Most business people who had flown in to meet with her had also flown out the same day. This was a situation that she hadn't quite anticipated.

She stepped forward and held out her hand to take his bag, but he resisted. She didn't know if he was being gentlemanly or if he was afraid that she might drop it. *Whatever.*

Once he placed the bag in the back of the cart, he joined her up front. His bicep brushed against her shoulder. It was as though static electricity flowed through her body. And suddenly the cart felt as though it had shrunk to half its size. Her mouth grew dry as her palms grew damp.

She refused to turn to him. Their faces would be far too close together. And there was something about his mouth that made her wonder if he had to be in control even when he was kissing someone. And then realizing how out of hand her thoughts had gotten, she gave herself a mental shake as she started the engine and then pressed on the accelerator.

She had to keep it together. She had to be a professional instead of letting the lack of a love life get the best of her. After all, the future of Infinity Island rested on her making this deal. And so they set off.

It was late afternoon by the time she'd given him the full tour. He was the first potential investor who had stuck around this long. Lea's hopes soared. He had many questions about the island and she did her best to answer them. She was proud of her little island. As she'd spoken of the various aspects of the island, Mr. Marinakos made notes on his digital tablet.

This is going to work. This is going to work.

She struggled not to grin. After all, nothing was final yet—

"Miss Romes, I'd like to make you an offer."
Yes! Yes! Yes!

She stifled the giddy happiness bubbling up inside her. She had to maintain her cool just a little longer. Later she could celebrate her success with Popi.

"Please call me Lea." When he sent her a puzzled look, she added, "If we're going to do business together, there's no need to stand on formality."

He hesitated. "Agreed. Call me Xander."

"Okay, Xander." She sent him her brightest smile. "What do you have in mind?"

And then he stated the most amazing number. She never ever imagined that anyone would want to invest such an incredible amount of money in the island. She wasn't even sure what to do with that much money. Sure the place needed work, but none that would amount to that sum.

"Thank you. That is a very generous investment—"

"Wait. I think you misunderstood me. I'm not investing in your island. I'm buying it."

He wanted to buy her island? Her heritage? Her heart sank clear down to her white sandals. This partnership was over before it even had a chance to begin.

Lea shook her head. This couldn't be happening. She'd only just found this link to her past, and she wasn't about to give it up. No way.

* * *

Xander Marinakos could feel this deal slipping through his fingers.

That was a very foreign position for him to be in.

The stubborn look on Lea's face said she wasn't giving up this island. And part of him applauded her while the rest of him thought it was a foolish endeavor. But he wasn't a man used to walking away empty-handed.

"If you're holding out for a better deal, you won't get one from me or anyone else. That's my one and only offer." He wasn't one to be trifled with—no matter how gorgeous he found this woman. Business was business.

"I'm afraid you came here under a false assumption. The island never was and never will be for sale."

His lips pressed into a firm line. He wondered if she even considered what she could do with the money he was offering her.

This island could be the jewel in his real estate empire. It was beautiful and so private. And yet, it wasn't that far off the mainland. Talk about a perfect location. He could build the most opulent estates that would sell for outrageous fortunes. He might even build a vacation home for himself. Not that he ever took vacations. But maybe someday he'd start.

"Is there anything I can say to change your mind?" If it was within reason, he'd consider it.

She didn't even hesitate when she gave another firm shake of her head. "This island has been in my family for generations and I intend to keep it that way."

He sighed. He was smart enough to know when to walk away. "Do me a favor?"

"What would that be?"

"If you ever change your mind about selling, let me know. This place would make a wonderful locale for exclusive estates."

She didn't look impressed. "It's already a noted wedding and honeymoon destination."

He didn't want to argue with her. He'd never heard of the island before it was brought to his attention as a potential building site, but then again, he avoided anything to do with happily-ever-afters. However, he refrained from mentioning it to Lea. He liked it better when she smiled. "So it is."

Though the grounds were well maintained, the place needed to be moved out of the last century and into the current one as far as technology and decorating went. He just didn't see anyone coming in here and wanting to invest in the place to develop it as a venue for weddings—not when there were so many other more lucrative uses for the island.

He stared into her blue-green eyes, seeing the depths of her desperation. But no one could truly help her until she realized that fixing this wedding island was a waste of money. And as a respectable businessman with his thumb on the heartbeat of development, he couldn't in good conscience throw good money after bad. It wasn't like love lasted. If it existed, it was fleeting at best.

"I suppose you won't be staying for the night." Lea's voice held a disappointed tone.

"Actually, you made the island sound so appealing that I'd like to stay for the night." He had made no plans for the evening or the next morning as he'd thought that he'd be hammering out a formative agreement.

"Not a problem at all." She turned from her position by the rail overlooking the cove, where the sun was starting its descent toward the horizon. "I can show you to your bungalow."

He liked Lea. She was pleasant, and when she smiled, her whole face lit up. And it had been a long time since he'd taken time for a social life. He'd prided himself on being able to amass his fortune before the age of thirty-five. But it had come at a price—his work schedule meant he hardly had a normal life.

There was something about this island—something so relaxing. Or perhaps it was the company. His gaze met hers. "I hope that even though we couldn't do business together we can still be friends."

Surprise lit up her eyes, but in a blink it was gone. "Um…sure. No hard feelings."

"Good. Would you care to join me for an early dinner?" When she hesitated, he added, "I'd love to hear more stories of the island and tales of your most outlandish weddings."

Her beautiful eyes widened. Was sharing a meal really that unusual for her? Or was she surprised by his interest in the goings-on of this eventful island? But with their business concluded, this meal would be…well, it would be between friends. He liked Lea, and the way she told stories was genuinely entertaining.

"Unless, of course, you have other plans." He hadn't considered that. "Perhaps with your husband or boyfriend?"

She shook her head. "I'm single."

"Good." And then realizing how that might sound, he added, "I mean that you're available for dinner."

"You don't have to pretend that you're interested in my stories—"

"There's no pretending. It's been a long time since I've been so amused. And by stories of goats, no less." He gestured for her to lead the way. "Shall we go?"

"Um…yes. The Hideaway Café is right this way."

In less than two minutes, they were at the restaurant. There was a thatched roof, ceiling fans and lots of colorful art on the walls. The aroma of coffee wafted through the air.

Xander loosened his tie. Then on second thought, he slipped it off and undid the top buttons on his dress shirt. It'd been a long time since he let himself enjoy a woman's company.

To his enjoyment, they were escorted to a patio table. It was just too nice a day to be stuck inside. Most of his life was spent in offices. This was different. And when his gaze came to rest on Lea, he decided that it was very nice indeed.

Once they'd ordered the food, he leaned back in his chair to take in the scenery. The very beautiful—very tempting—scenery. He couldn't take his eyes off her. Lea was someone he longed to know so much better.

"I never expected to find someone so—" He stopped himself from saying "beautiful" and instead said, "...so young running the island. By your accent, I'm guessing you're not from Greece."

"I'm not. I grew up in Seattle."

"That's a long way from here. So why move here? Why give up everything to run a wedding island?"

She fidgeted with a spoon on the table. "Because I wanted to learn more about my heritage. Do you know why they call this Infinity Island?"

He shook his head.

"Because when two hearts are joined here, they are joined for infinity. Not for a year or two or ten. It's forever. That's why we're selective with our clientele. The happy couples that marry here come from all around the world."

"And if you weren't so choosy, you might not be in such a dire situation. You could have more than one wedding a week. There wouldn't be any downtime like now."

She frowned at him. "We aren't in it for the money. This island is special and I won't part with it for you to build some expensive homes for people that don't understand the significance of the island and its history."

"You speak like you've lived here your entire life."

"Sometimes it feels that way." She never made any secret about her past. "My mother left Greece when she fell in love with an American soldier. She followed him to the States, where I came to be."

"So how did you end up back here?"

"My aunt never had any children of her own. I was her sole heir and she entrusted me with the island."

"What about your mother?"

"She and my father still live in the States on a little island off the Pacific coast. My mother, well, she had a falling-out with her family."

"I probably shouldn't do this since I'd really like it if you would call me in the near future and sell me the island, but I have some advice to keep your business afloat."

Her eyes lit up with interest. "What would that be?"

"This place is practically empty." He waved around at the plethora of empty tables. "Open the island up to vacationers as well as wedding guests. It would keep a steady flow of people and increase the flow of revenue."

"I'll keep that in mind."

But he could tell she'd already considered the option and dismissed it. Apparently traditions ran deep where this island was concerned. Xander couldn't help but wonder if it was really the love of the island or if there was something else keeping her here away from her family—away from society.

But he kept those questions to himself as they savored a delightful array of fresh vegetables, seafood and cheeses produced on the island. The meal was leisurely and the food was out of this world. He was quite tempted to lure the chef away and put him on staff at the Skyrise Restaurant atop his headquarters in Athens.

Even though the sun had slipped below the horizon, leaving a pink hue in its wake, Xander wasn't ready to end his time with Lea.

They strolled down to the beach. No one was around, and they enjoyed the surf and sand alone.

"I really should get back to work," Lea said, but her voice lacked desire.

"I should, too. But why don't we play hooky this evening?"

She glanced at him as they ambled along the shore. "Do you usually play hooky?"

"No."

"Then why this evening?"

He stopped and turned to her. "Because you reminded me that there is so much more to life than business. I haven't laughed this much…ever. It has been a truly wonderful evening." He stared deep into her eyes. "I don't want it to end."

"You don't?"

"I don't." His gaze lowered to her lips. They were so inviting. He'd been glancing at them off and on all through dinner. They were rosy and glossy. Nothing about her appearance was overly done. She was more down-to-earth and much more appealing than any of the women he'd dated in the past.

He had a policy of not mixing business and pleasure. Tonight, he might have been tempted to break that long-standing rule, but he knew Lea wasn't going to change her mind about his offer. And so there was no reason to hold back. They could find out where the evening would take them.

He stepped closer, watching and waiting to see if she would pull away. She didn't. He glanced down, catching the slight pulse in her neck. She was as intrigued by him as he was by her. The most captivating thing about her wasn't her gorgeous face or luscious lips, but the beauty inside that glowed outward.

He reached out to her. His movements were slow so as not to startle her. And then his fingers caressed her smooth, soft cheek. "You are the most incredible woman I've met."

There was an audible hiss as she sucked her breath in through her teeth. Her eyes widened and then took on an inviting look. He had no intention of missing out on such a tempting invitation.

He lowered his head, but before he got very far, she was there—meeting him in the middle. Her tender lips pressed to his. The breath caught in the back of his throat. Her touch was like a static charge—sending a current through his body, making every cell vibrate with desire.

His hand lowered to her waist. He drew her to him. Her hands came to rest on his chest as their kiss deepened. He hadn't ventured to Infinity Island with a thought of having a romantic tryst—not at all. He'd been disappointed that he hadn't been able to purchase the island, but this wasn't so bad as a consolation prize. And though he'd deny it to anyone, he'd ended up with the better of the two options.

The more he tasted Lea, the more he wanted her. She snuggled up against him. Her soft, voluptuous curves fit perfectly against him. He had a feeling this evening was only going to get better and better.

CHAPTER ONE

Late June...

TWO PINK LINES...

Three separate results...

Diagnosis: Pregnant.

Every time Lea thought about it, which was quite often, she started to hyperventilate. This couldn't be happening. Not now. Not when her life was in such an uproar.

But she'd had all of the early symptoms, from her missed cycle to tender breasts. As much as she wanted to live in the land of denial, she couldn't. There was now a baby to take into consideration. And a man who didn't have a clue he was about to become a father. Well, he would if he'd answer his phone.

After a trip to the doctor for official confirmation, Lea had tried repeatedly to reach Xander and let him know she was pregnant, not because she wanted anything from him but because it was the right thing to do. But each time she called, it went straight to voice mail. It wasn't until she tracked down the number to his office in Athens that she learned he was out of the country on business.

So once again, she called him. Once again, her

call was forwarded to voice mail. "Xander, this is Lea. Um…" Her stomach churned with nerves even though he wasn't on the other end of the line. "I need to talk to you. Could you give me a call when you get a chance?"

She pressed the end button on her phone and took her first full breath. And then she realized that "when you get a chance" probably didn't convey the urgency that she felt or the importance of the news she had to tell him. Still, it was better than nothing. He would get back to her soon. Until then she had an island to save and a baby to prepare for. Plenty of things to keep her mind off Xander…as if that was possible.

He listened to the voice mail.

And then he listened to it again.

Xander could tell there was something off in Lea's voice, but he couldn't quite narrow down the problem or determined if there even was one. And then he realized what it must be—she was disappointed that he hadn't phoned her. Not that the thought hadn't crossed his mind more than a few times.

In fact, he hadn't been able to get Lea off of his mind since their lost weekend in paradise. Random memories of her distracted him from his work and filled his dreams at night. She was an amazing woman, not only in looks but in everything about her. It was so tempting to pick up the phone and call her back. If it were possible, he'd drop everything and return to Infinity Island. But his busy life didn't allow for such indulgences.

At first, he hadn't believed it, but by the time he departed Infinity Island, he knew there was something extra special about it—about Lea. Maybe he'd let himself get caught up in the most amazing views of the sea or the tranquil cove or even the colorful vegetation. Or more likely it was letting his guard down with Lea and enjoying the moment that had him so distracted from his work.

But right now, he was fully involved in a resort deal with his younger sister, Stasia. It was their first business deal together. And with his sister at loose ends after losing her husband, Xander was willing to do whatever he could for her.

And his sister, against his recommendation, had risked her entire life's savings on this project being a success. That was a responsibility he didn't want, but being stubborn and insistent, Stasia had put him in that very unwelcome position.

As much as he would like to see Lea again, it would have to wait for quite a while. Business came first. It always had. And it always would. Except when family shoved their way to the front of his priorities. Of course, his sister knew how much he adored her. He would do anything for her. And the feeling was mutual.

He set aside his phone and loosened his tie. His trip to the interior of Asia had not been fruitful. He'd known that it would be a long shot from the start, but long shots were what had catapulted him to the top of his field. Sometimes leads panned out and other times, well, they were a waste of time. But it never stopped him from seeking out the next big deal, in some of the most unlikely places.

He'd just hung up his tie in his walk-in closet that was the size of a second bedroom when he heard his phone buzz. He was really quite tempted to let it go to voice mail. He'd been traveling all day and what he longed for was a hot shower to ease the tension in his neck. But he had been out of contact for an extensive amount of time... and this could be important.

With a deep sigh, Xander headed back into the bedroom. On the way, he loosened the top buttons on his white dress shirt. He glanced down at the phone and was surprised to find Lea's name on the caller ID. She was calling again? That struck him as odd.

Sure, he hadn't known her that long, but she didn't strike him as the pushy type. In fact, she seemed quite the opposite. And she was more than willing to stand on her own two feet. Was it possible that he'd incorrectly interpreted her earlier voice mail?

Not giving himself time to think about it further, he answered the call. "Lea, how are you?"

"Xander, finally. I've been trying to reach you for a while now. I was beginning to think that you were avoiding my calls—"

"Whoa. Slow down." Something really had her worked up. "I just got home a few minutes ago. What's wrong?"

"I… I don't know if you'd say it's wrong or not."

"Just tell me what it is and we'll go from there."

There was an extended pause. He could imagine her worrying her bottom lip, like she did when she was unsure of something. While he'd been on Infinity Island, he'd picked up on her mannerisms. He found her quite captivating. It was one of the reasons he'd avoided calling her. He knew if she asked him to return to the island, it would be too great a temptation.

As the silence dragged on, Xander said, "Lea, I can't help until you tell me what's the matter."

"I'm pregnant."

Xander stumbled back as though her words had physically slugged him in the chest. The back of his knees hit the edge of the bed. He slumped down onto the mattress. Maybe he'd heard her incorrectly.

"Could you say that again?"

"Xander, I'm pregnant. And you're the father."

That was what he thought she'd said.

But this can't be true. Could it?

Xander knew all too well that it was quite possible. They'd spent that not-so-long-ago weekend in bed…and there was the time on the floor…in the living room—

He halted his rambling memories. He didn't normally let loose like that. In fact, he'd never had a weekend like that one. It was unforgettable. And apparently in more than one way.

But he had to be absolutely sure of what he heard. "Could you say that again?"

"I'm pregnant."

His heart pounded so loud that it echoed in his ears. As though all the energy had been drained from his body, he fell back on the bed. His fingers combed through his hair as his palm rubbed against his forehead, where a throbbing headache was starting.

The silence grew heavy. He should say something. Anything. But what? He'd never been in this position before.

He needed time to think because right now all that was going around in his mind was that he was going to be a father. He wondered if this was what shock felt like.

"I… I need a little time to absorb this," he said. "We'll talk soon."

He wasn't even sure if he said goodbye before disconnecting the call. He had no idea how long he lay there staring into space before the buzz of an incoming text jarred him back to reality.

I'm going to be a father.

The profound words echoed in his mind.

How could this be? Well, of course he knew how it happened. It was a weekend that he would never forget, much as he had tried. Lea's stunning image was imprinted upon his mind.

Still, he'd never thought he'd hear that he was going to be a father.

A father.

Those two little words sent his heart racing as his palms grew damp. His mind slipped back to the time he'd spent on Infinity Island. He'd never expected it to change his life. But it had. And now he had to figure out a plan. He was known for thinking on his toes, but this was different. This was a baby. His baby.

And he had to do whatever was best for the child.

But what was that?

CHAPTER TWO

HAD HE BEEN STUNNED?

Was that why he'd ended the phone call so quickly?

Maybe he'd been in shock. He had said that they'd talk soon. What exactly did *soon* mean?

The next day Lea was still playing over her conversation with Xander. It had ended so abruptly that it startled her. She didn't know what she'd been expecting, but it hadn't been for him to become so quiet. Perhaps she'd been waiting for him to lob questions and accusations but none of that had come.

Did he outright not believe her? She knew that was always a possibility, but she just wanted to believe that Xander was more of a man than to shirk his responsibilities. Granted she didn't know him that well, but she sensed he was a good guy—a man who cared for those closest to him—even if to the world he portrayed himself as a ruthless businessman. In private, he was a very different man. That much she was certain about.

Or the other possibility—the one that she was going with—was that she had absolutely blindsided him with the news of the baby. How could he not be shocked? She certainly had been. A baby was the last thing she'd had on her mind at the moment. Her priority had been trying to keep a roof over her head in the upcoming year.

She sighed, not about the baby but about the state of the island. She straightened up the papers on her office desk. She felt as though she were letting down her family, which was silly when you thought of it, because she didn't know any of the people who had run the island before her. And her parents, well, they wanted nothing to do with the island. So perhaps she felt as though she were letting down herself.

When she first learned that she'd inherited this gorgeous island, she'd imagined swooping in here and making it the best—the most shiny, sought-after wedding destination. Instead she was patching holes, painting walls and duct-taping hoses. Half of the guest rooms were shut down due to one reason or another.

In addition, she'd had to reduce the staff. As a result, she'd had to take on additional responsibilities that took up any free time and had her falling into bed at night utterly exhausted.

She stood and moved out from behind her desk that still had a slew of unfinished tasks. A more urgent problem needed her attention. A leaking faucet. Thankfully her parents had had no gender bias when raising her. She used to assist her father with all sorts of tasks around the house—including plumbing.

Lea moved to the closet, opened the door and retrieved a red toolbox. She almost felt as though she needed a tool belt to sling around her waist—to give her that authentic fixer-lady look. She wondered what Xander would make of the look. A giggle rose in her throat as she imagined a horrified look on his handsome face.

Dressed in a loose T-shirt and a pair of old jean shorts that had the top button loosened to make room for her expanding midsection, she set off for the bungalow midway across the island. She hoped it was just a worn-out washer and nothing more serious. She had a big wedding this weekend. She couldn't afford to lose yet another accommodation because there was nowhere else to house people unless she gave up her bungalow.

She'd just placed the toolbox in the golf cart when she heard the whoop-whoop of a helicopter. This couldn't be good. They weren't expecting any new guests today.

The people on the island either lived and worked there or were lingering guests from the past weekend's wedding. There was also a couple celebrating their fiftieth anniversary. Some of their guests liked to return every year for their anniversary, sort of as a reminder of how it felt when their love had been so new, fresh and exciting.

She worried her bottom lip. Could it be a medical emergency? No. She would have been informed.

But as the warm breeze caressed her skin, she put a hand to her forehead, blocking the bright sunshine. She tilted her chin upward to watch the helicopter descend to the helipad not far from her office. Whoever this was, they weren't a guest.

Her body tensed as the long seconds dragged out. She never knew it could take so long for a chopper to land. But she knew that in reality not much time had passed at all. It was just her anxiety that seemed to have slowed the world down as she waited to see what new problem awaited her.

And then the door to the helicopter opened. And…

The breath of anticipation hitched in her throat. And…

A man emerged from inside. His head was ducked, but he had dark hair. And his clothes appeared to be a business suit. Her heart plummeted to her tennis shoes. Could this be an attorney putting some sort of lien against the island as she wasn't quite on top of all of her bills. She tried. But some months she had to pay some accounts and then the next month she paid others.

But as the man rushed away from the helipad, there was something familiar about him. She couldn't put her finger on what exactly it was, but she sensed she knew him. And then as the man reached the steps leading away from the helipad, he lifted his head.

A breath hissed past Lea's teeth. *Xander.* She blinked. He was still there and he was staring directly at her.

She sucked in a deep breath, pulling in her baby bump, but that only succeeded in making her ever-expanding breasts stick out even further. She immediately released the pent-up breath. There was no hiding that her body was changing.

What was he doing here? And then she realized that in her shock, she'd asked the most ridiculous question. He wasn't here to see her—not like she'd dreamed about at night where they'd rushed into each other's arms. No, he was here about her baby—their baby.

She'd only told him the news yesterday. She couldn't believe he was standing in front of her. But he was looking a little out of sorts. His necktie was missing. His collar was loosened. He hadn't shaved, leaving a dark shadow of stubble to highlight his squared jaw.

It was then that she noticed he wasn't smiling as he made his way to her. If he wasn't happy about the baby, why bother coming? It wasn't like she'd placed any demands upon him. She wasn't poor, even if the state of the island said otherwise. This land was worth a lot of money—he'd pointed that out to her. If the absolute worst happened, she could sell the island and live comfortably the rest of her life. But she would have to be desperate to sell her heritage. At this point, she wasn't desperate. At least that was what she kept telling herself.

Hang in there. This is all going to work out.

She wondered if the pep speech was about the dire state of the island or about her impending meeting with Xander. She hadn't moved since she'd watched him arrive. Normally she would have met a guest halfway, but not today—not with Xander frowning. She had to be strong and stand her ground. He could come to her.

When Xander finally stopped in front of her, she stood silently. Her stomach churned nervously. She hadn't invited him here. It was up to him to decide how this conversation should go.

"I'm here." He stared at her with tired eyes.

That's it? That's all he has to say?

She leveled her shoulders and tilted her chin upward. "I didn't ask you to come. We could have handled this over the phone."

"This is too serious for a phone call."

But with a phone call, she would have been able to concentrate on the conversation instead of how he looked even sexier than she recalled. She fidgeted with the gemstone bracelet on her wrist before forcing her hands to remain still at her sides.

This conversation definitely would have gone

smoother over the phone. As soon as she would have assured him that she wasn't plotting a messy paternity or support lawsuit, they could have gotten back to their lives. Because she could do this parenting thing on her own. In fact, she was looking forward to being a mother.

When Lea noticed him staring expectantly at her, she said, "I thought you'd be busy with work."

A definite note of incredulity clung to his voice. "You can't just deliver a bombshell, over the phone no less, and expect me to do nothing."

"What do you want to know?"

"How about for starters, are you sure the baby is mine?" His gaze narrowed as he stared at her as though by look alone he could ferret out the truth.

The fact that he would question her about something so important hurt—it hurt deeply. Apparently they didn't know each other at all. The weekend they'd spent in each other's company for every exquisite moment had meant more to her than him. So be it.

"Yes. I'm sure." If he thought she was going to stand here in public to be interrogated, he was mistaken. "I have to go. I have an emergency."

Without giving him a chance to respond, she turned back to the golf cart. She climbed inside and started it. She glanced up and was about to put her foot on the accelerator when she found him standing directly in her path, with his arms crossed over his broad chest and a definite frown on his face.

She sighed. "I don't want to fight with you. In fact, I don't want anything from you."

"Then why call?"

Seriously? He had to ask that?

And then one of the staff started in their direction. The man was giving them a strange look as though trying to decide whether he should step in or not. She made a point of painting a friendly smile on her face and waving at her employee. The man smiled, nodded and kept moving.

Lea turned back to Xander. "Would you stop standing there like some Greek statue and get in?" When he didn't move, she said, "Xander, don't make a scene."

Without a word, he climbed in beside her. His shoulder brushed up against hers, sending a wave of nervous energy racing through her body. It settled in her chest. As she breathed in his spicy aftershave, the heat in her chest gravitated southward to her core. Her back teeth ground together, refusing to give in to her body's desires. That boat had sailed. It was out of the docks, out of the harbor, and was headed into open seas.

CHAPTER THREE

His quietness was unnerving.

Lea sent Xander a sideways glance. The set of his jaw and the twitch in his cheek let her know that he was angry. Sitting so close to him, she could feel the agitation radiating off him.

She didn't know what gave him the right to be so upset. It wasn't like she'd ended up in this condition by herself. It definitely took two to tango. If she'd hidden the baby from him, it would be different. But that hadn't happened. And lastly, she didn't expect or request a thing from him. So if he wanted to be mad at her, he could just sit there and stew. She had work to do.

Lea slowed the golf cart to a stop outside the honeymoon bungalow. Without a word, she got out. She grabbed her toolbox with a replacement rubber washer in it and headed up the four wooden steps to the front door.

The guests were supposed to have checked out by now, but as was standard procedure on the island, Lea rapped her knuckles soundly on the door. "Hello. Maintenance."

A moment passed with no response.

She lifted her hand to insert her passkey but missed. If only Xander would go away, the slight tremble in her hands would stop. Lea inhaled a deep breath and tried again. This time she got it.

Footsteps sounded behind her. She didn't have to turn to know it was Xander. She could smell the faint whiff of his cologne mingled with his male scent. It was an intoxicating combination.

Ignoring Xander, Lea opened the door slowly so as not to startle anyone that may be lingering on the inside. "Hello. Anyone here?" She glanced around for any sign of guests. "Maintenance coming in."

With the door wide open, she stepped inside. No people. No luggage. No discarded dishes or drinks in the living room area or the kitchenette. They were alone—

Alone with Xander in a honeymoon bungalow. What made her think bringing him along was a good idea? Oh, yeah, he hadn't given her a choice.

Then the door snicked shut behind her. She glanced over her shoulder, her gaze verifying that the door was indeed closed and then registering that Xander was standing very close to her. So close she could reach back and place her hand upon his chest. She swallowed hard and resisted the temptation.

So as not to give into her impulse, she faced forward, as though by turning away she'd be able to forget just how sexy he looked. In her mind, she pictured him clearly in that navy blue suit, sans tie and with the top buttons of his light blue dress shirt undone, giving a hint of the few dark curls on his chest. Lea stifled a moan.

On stilted legs, she headed toward the master suite. Her heart was racing. Her palms were damp. How was she ever going to be able to work with him lurking over her shoulder?

She stopped before reaching the bedroom. "You can take the golf cart and head back to the offices." She was getting desperate for some space— a chance to think clearly. "I can walk. It'll be good for the baby."

"Why would I do that?"

Because you're making me a nervous wreck.

Lea moistened her dry lips. "I didn't think you'd want to stick around and watch me fix a leaky faucet."

"Why are you doing maintenance work? Don't you have people to do those sorts of things? I mean in your condition, should you be doing manual labor?"

She turned a narrow gaze on him. "I'm pregnant, not dying. And now that the morning sickness has passed, I have a lot of energy." She tilted up her chin. "Trust me, I won't do anything that would endanger the baby."

He nodded in understanding. "I still don't understand why you're doing this."

She didn't want to tell him just how bad off the

island was these days. With more and more accommodations shut down because of needed repairs, the fewer weddings she could book. The fewer weddings booked, the less income for repairs. It was one big downward spiral and she had yet to find a way to stop it. If only she could find an investor who didn't want to change the island or the way the business was run. But so far, she hadn't found that right person. And it certainly wasn't Xander, who wanted to rip down everything her ancestors had built and loved.

"That's not the kind of owner I am. I like to be a part of everything. Make sure things are functioning properly."

He arched a brow. "And you can tell all of that by fixing a faucet?"

His tone let her know he didn't believe her. But that was his problem. She didn't have time to alleviate his curiosity. She had work to do. And this was her best unit on the island.

When she reached the master bedroom, she immediately stepped in water. It seeped up over her sandals. The breath hitched in her throat, smothering a scream.

A little leak? A drippy faucet?

Lea muttered under her breath as she rushed toward the bathroom. Her foot slipped on the wet floor. The next thing she knew, she was falling back. Strong hands reached out and caught her.

She didn't have time to thank him, she had to shut off the water.

Inside the bathroom, oblivious to the water, she knelt down and leaned under the countertop. She tried the shutoff valve under the sink but it wouldn't budge. Using her whole-body strength, she groaned, but the valve didn't move at all.

"Here. Let me try," Xander said from behind her.

She turned to him and was about to tell him that this wasn't his problem, when she noticed he'd divested himself of his suit coat. It now hung over the towel rack and his shirtsleeves were rolled up.

He held a hand out to her. "Hurry up. The water is still pouring in."

He was right. This was not the time to stand on pride. If she lost this unit, the island would go out of business and her heritage would be lost. She couldn't let that happen. It was her job to protect her family's legacy—something her mother refused to do.

Lea watched as he clenched the wrench. The corded muscles of his forearms strained. His neck grew taut as his lips pressed together in a firm line. A deep groan filled the room as he gave it everything to move the valve.

After a few failed attempts, he turned to her. "Where's the main water shutoff for the whole unit?"

"Outside. In the back, I think." Up until this point, she hadn't had any need to turn off the water main, but she knew the bulk of the units had the utility hookup in the back, out of view from the guests.

Xander stood. The water dripped off him—his suit was going to be ruined. And then she noticed his black leather dress shoes. They were partially submerged in water. Lea inwardly groaned as she thought of how many hundreds or more likely thousands of dollars his attire cost—something she didn't have the extra cash to replace. She would have to deal with that later.

She took off for the door with Xander hot on her heels. The water shutoff thankfully was easy to find. And unlike the valve inside, it turned pretty easily.

Turning the water off was only the first step in fixing this huge mess. They rushed back inside, using everything available to mop up the water from the floor. Xander opened all of the windows. They continued to work together in peaceful harmony.

When the last of the water had been mopped up, Lea stood and inspected the damage. Thankfully the wood floor wasn't discolored. It didn't look like the water had been there long. Lea thanked her lucky stars.

As she placed the last wet towel in a laundry

bag, she turned to Xander, who had just gotten to his feet after checking the plumbing joint under the sink. "Thank you."

"No problem."

Her gaze took in his wet, wrinkled suit. "I think your clothes are ruined."

He glanced down as though he'd forgotten he was wearing dress clothes. "I've got more."

"I didn't see any luggage."

"True. Everything is back in Athens. I was in a bit of a hurry."

"Obviously." She gave it a little thought. "Let's drop off these wet linens and then we'll get you something dry to wear."

He gave her a strange look. "I don't think you'll have anything that will fit me."

His words inspired an image of him in women's clothes and a smile pulled at her lips. As they climbed in the golf cart, the image of Xander wearing her clothes wouldn't leave her. She pressed on the accelerator.

"You're picturing me in your clothes, aren't you?"

"I…uh…no, I'm not." But she couldn't subdue her amusement.

"You are. I know it. But trust me, nothing you have would fit me."

The frown on his face only added to her amusement. She knew that after the disaster at the bungalow she shouldn't be smiling, much less laughing, but she couldn't help herself. The laughter bubbled out of her.

Maybe it was some strange reaction to stress. Or perhaps it was her pregnancy hormones. Whatever it was, she couldn't stop laughing. And looking in Xander's direction only made it worse.

"What?" he asked as his frown deepened. "Do I have something on me?" He then started to wipe his face off. "Would you stop that?"

"I'm trying." Lea did her best to subdue her unexpected amusement. "It's not you."

He arched a dark brow. "Then why are you laughing at me?"

She shook her head. "I'm not."

"Sure seems like it to me."

"I've just never seen someone in expensive clothes crawling around on a flooded floor." She dabbed at her damp eyes. "You're a mess."

"And that's funny?"

"No. Not really." The grumpier he became the cuter he got. That acknowledgment sobered Lea. Being attracted to him was what had gotten them in this situation in the first place. "Anyway. What are you doing here?"

"You need to ask?"

"Apparently I do or I wouldn't have asked you."

She pulled the golf cart to a stop in front of her bungalow—the same place that their baby was conceived. It was as though they'd come full circle and were now back at the beginning. She got out and headed for the door.

She glanced over her shoulder, finding Xander still sitting in the cart. "Come on. You can't go around looking like that all day."

She let herself inside the small but airy bungalow, lit abundantly from the floor-to-ceiling windows. She wasn't quite sure how to act around Xander. It wasn't as though they were strangers, but there was definitely a thick layer of awkwardness between them.

"The shower is through there." She pointed to the guest bathroom.

He looked at her. "Are you sure you don't want to get one first?"

She glanced down at herself. She was as wet as him, with some black grease marks here and there.

Her hand moved to her hair. It was still damp on the ends and the rest of it was growing frizzy. She must look a sight. No one would desire her in this state. And that was for the best. She tried to tell herself that she was relieved but what she was really feeling was disappointment.

Not wanting to dwell on her disheveled appearance, she grabbed her purse from the side of the couch and headed for the front door. "I'll be back shortly."

"Where are you going?"

"To get you something to wear." Not waiting for his response, she strode outside, pulling the door shut behind her.

There was only a limited number of retail shops on the island. Most people who visited weren't interested in shopping, except for the occasional necessity. But they did have a boutique and that was where Lea headed.

The only problem was that everything in the island boutique was geared to leisurely, fun-in-the-sun clothes. There were no suits, not even jeans because it was hot outside with only the sea breeze to cool you off. There was actually a pair of gray sweats lurking on the back shelf, but Lea dismissed them. Xander would melt in them.

She moved on to a pair of navy shorts with a white anchor pattern. This was more like it. Her mind filled with an image of Xander in them, showing off his well-defined calf muscles. The man was a walking advertisement for the benefit of working out daily.

She picked up a white T-shirt with *Infinity Island* emblazed across the front of it. Her gaze moved to the section of the shop with the more intimate items, but there was no way she was buying him underwear. Not a chance. She had to draw the line somewhere.

She started for the checkout but realized she was being silly. If she could have his baby, she could pick out some boxers. Still, it felt like something a girlfriend or, dare she say it, a wife would do. As she scanned over the various colors and styles, her mind conjured up images of Xander wearing them.

She resisted the urge to fan herself. Boy, was it getting warm in here. Eager to get this over with, she grabbed a few pairs of extra-large boxers. If he wanted something else, he could come here and shop for himself. With her face still warm, she started for the front of the store, passing by the rack of flip-flops. She grabbed a pair. He would be all set to go—to go home to Athens.

With her purchase made, Lea headed back to her place. Soon Xander would be gone and then she could relax. She glanced at the time. The once-a-day ferry would be arriving at lunchtime and he could hitch a ride back to the mainland. Whatever he'd hoped to accomplish by coming here wasn't going to happen.

He had his life.

And she had hers.

Could they stay in contact for their child? If he wanted. She didn't have any qualms about updating him on the progress of the pregnancy.

And that was exactly what she planned to tell him when she entered the bungalow. She dropped her purse on the living room couch and moved to the guest room. She knocked on the open door but got no response. It was then that she noticed the sound of running water. She moved to the bed, hoping to leave the clothes there and get out before he came out of the shower. She'd just placed the bag from the boutique on the bed when Xander emerged from the bathroom.

A billow of steam surrounded him like he was some Greek god. His hair was still wet and spiky. His face and shoulders were damp. And beads of water trailed down over his muscled chest before being absorbed by the fluffy pink towel slung low over his trim hips.

Lea swallowed hard. It was like having her very own hot-guys calendar come to life—not that she had such a calendar. But after seeing Xander, the idea was tempting. So long as he was in it. But then she knew she'd never switch the month. It'd always be Xander's month.

He cleared his throat, drawing her gaze upward. "Is that for me?"

Heat rushed from her chest to her face, scorching her cheeks. With great reluctance, she glanced away. "Yes, there are some, uh, clothes. They should fit." And then realizing she shouldn't be here at this particularly awkward moment, she said, "I'll, um, wait for you in the living room."

"There's no need for you to run off." A knowing smile lit up his face.

But Lea didn't look back and didn't pause until

she'd reached the kitchen sink. Noticing that her mouth was parched, she grabbed a drinking glass from the cabinet and filled it with some ice-cold water from the fridge. She downed the entire thing in one long gulp, but it did nothing to cool her down. Thankfully he would soon be on that boat and out of her space. Not much longer now.

"Thanks for the clothes." Xander's voice came from behind her. "But you didn't have to."

"It's the least I could do—" The words died in her throat as she turned to him. On second thought, she should have gone with the sweat suit. Then he'd be just as uncomfortably warm as her.

The T-shirt barely fit him as it was pulled tight over his broad shoulders and chest. The man could probably lift one of her in each hand without breaking a sweat. His waist was narrow. And the shorts didn't hang as low as she'd have thought. She definitely had a view of his legs—legs that weren't tanned. Her gaze moved to his arms. They weren't tanned, either. The man definitely spent too much time in a suit.

She could ask him to stay. He obviously needed some downtime in the sun. But that was not a good idea. She did not need any more complications.

He moved to the couch and sat down. "No more distractions. We need to talk."

He was right. It was time to get it all out there in the open. "I don't expect anything from you if that's what you're worried about. I can take care of the baby."

He patted the couch cushion next to him. "Come over here."

She didn't trust herself being so close to that sexy hunk of a man, but she refused to let on that he still got under her skin. She forced her feet one in front of the other. She perched on the edge of the couch, leaving as much space between them as possible.

She could still remember how good his kisses were and how his hands created the most arousing sensations wherever he touched. The mere memories sent her heart racing. When her gaze met his, there was a challenge reflected in his eyes.

She glanced at the clock on the stove. "If you don't hurry, you'll miss the ferry. It's the only one today."

"Is this the way it's going to be?"

She turned her full attention to him. "How *what* is going to be?"

"You and me. How do I even know the baby is mine?"

"I'd like to think that no one would lie about such an important thing. But you obviously don't trust me. So after the baby is born, a test can be done. But there's no way I'm having one of those great big foot-long needles stabbed into my stomach." She visibly flinched at the memory of what she'd seen on the internet. She didn't like needles. They all looked huge to her.

"I want to trust you, but I've had people lie to me in the past about much smaller matters." Pain reflected in his eyes.

"It's understandable that you would want confirmation. It isn't like we've been in a loving, committed relationship."

His eyes widened. "Is that what you want? For us to marry for the sake of the child?"

"No." It was a short, straight-to-the-point answer.

His gaze narrowed. "Are you sure?"

Why was he pushing this so much? Surely he didn't think marriage was a good idea, did he? It was not even like they were in love. They were, well, they were friends at best. And not very good friends at that.

"I'm sure." Her tone was firm. "Besides, you don't have time for a family. You're always working."

"I can make time for everything—" Just then his phone buzzed and he retrieved it from his pocket.

"Point proven."

After nothing more than a glance, he returned the phone to his pocket. "So you're planning to do this all on your own?"

"If you mean raising the baby, then yes, I plan

to be a single parent. It's not like there are a lot of single guys on the island. Most are bridegrooms or a guest of a wedding party. They generally bring a date and don't flirt with the island staff."

"You're going to stay here on the island and raise the baby?"

"This is where my ancestors were born and raised. It's where my mother grew up. If it's good enough for them, it's good enough for me and the baby."

"And what about what happened today with the honeymoon bungalow?" he asked.

"What about it? Things break." She tried to brush off the incident as nothing out of the ordinary, but she knew it was a very big deal indeed.

He leaned forward, resting his elbows on his knees. "Don't act so blasé. I saw you earlier. You were practically in a panic. This island needs a lot of work—work that you don't have the money to do."

Her mouth gaped. *How dare he?* "Since when do you know about my finances?"

"Since I did some digging when I wanted to buy the island. I needed to know just what I was getting myself into."

She wanted to ask what he'd learned, but she didn't. Nothing good would come of it. Where finances were concerned Infinity Island was in disastrous straits.

Xander gazed into her eyes, making her heart race. "You need to rethink this—"

"Rethink what? Giving up my home? My past? My future?" She shook her head. "If you think you're going to talk me into selling you the island, it isn't going to happen. Remember? We already had this conversation."

"You don't have to stay here. I can set you up in Athens. Anywhere in the city. You name it."

She crossed her arms. "I'm not leaving the island."

"Stop being so stubborn and see what's right in front of you."

Her voice started to rise. "I do see it. And just because this place isn't perfect doesn't mean I should turn my back and walk away."

He sighed and got to his feet. Without another word, he started for the door.

"Where are you going?" she asked.

"Out." And with that he stepped onto the covered deck.

She should be relieved, but she wasn't. She felt like they'd talked about everything except what he really had on his mind. And then there was the whistle of the approaching ferry.

She rushed to the doorway. "You're going to miss your ride back to the mainland."

"I'm not leaving." He kept walking.

Not leaving? He made it sound like it would be

indefinitely, but she knew that couldn't be the case. He had a business empire to run.

She assured herself that he'd just be here for a day or two. Just long enough to figure out how this pregnancy would affect their lives. Then he'd go back to his life in Athens. And she would remain here on the island.

CHAPTER FOUR

WHAT EXACTLY WAS he supposed to do now?

Xander raked his fingers through his hair, not caring what it looked like. For once, his appearance would make no difference in the negotiation. Usually he made a point of looking on top of his game, with the finest suit, the best haircut and a clean shave. He liked to let his competitors know that he was used to winning—that he didn't accept being second best.

But dealing with Lea was totally different. Money didn't impress her. She understood its necessity to survive, but it wasn't her driving force. And that was something foreign to him. Since he'd been a teenager, he'd been focused on amassing a fortune. And now at the age of thirty-one, he had more money than he could possibly spend in this lifetime, but he still wasn't satisfied. He was still looking to make the next deal—something to fill the emptiness inside.

His gaze moved over the island. This time he wasn't taking in his surroundings the same way as he had during his prior visit. Before, his interest was in the landscape and the eventual demolition followed by its rebirth. This time he was looking to see what it would take to make this island viable as a wedding destination for the fore-seeable future.

He'd noticed the determined glint in Lea's eyes when he'd mentioned selling the island. It was the same look he imagined he had when he bought his first piece of property that had been uneven and heavily vegetated. His father had told him that he'd thrown away his money. Xander had secretly been having his own doubts, but his father's words had been like a challenge. Xander had done everything to clear and level that plot of land. In the end, he'd tripled his money. With the proceeds he'd bought more property.

Lea would stay here on Infinity Island and do whatever it took to keep the family business going—even if it took the last bit of money she possessed. And it would. Most of the structures needed new roofs. The landscaping needed to be reworked in places. The bungalows needed new windows and paint, and that was just scratching the surface.

He didn't know how long he'd walked—wearing off his frustration. In the process, he'd been trying to wrap his mind around the fact that he was going to be a father. He'd always thought fatherhood was something he didn't want, but now it was no longer a choice. He refused to turn his back on his baby like his biological parents had done to him when they'd left him on the steps in front of the hospital.

And though his adoptive parents had loved him,

it just hadn't been the same as what they felt for his sister—their flesh and blood. Growing up, he'd blamed himself—telling himself that he wasn't good enough. If he'd have just tried harder, they'd have loved him the same as they loved his sister. He'd never allowed any of them that chance.

Now he had a baby of his own. He would do whatever it took to see that Lea and the baby were taken care of. Money wouldn't be an issue.

If Lea insisted on remaining on the island, he could have the island all fixed up. And he would contact his financial planner to set up a trust fund for his son...or daughter. He liked the idea. At last, he had the beginnings of a plan.

As for being an involved father, he was less certain about it. With his past, he doubted he could be a loving parent. They'd all be better off if he remained in the shadows.

Xander pulled his phone out of his pocket and pressed the speed dial. The phone was answered on the first ring as though Roberto, his second-in-charge, was sitting there waiting for him to call. But of course, he wouldn't be because he had too many other things he should be doing.

Xander dispensed with the pleasantries and went straight for the important stuff. "Roberto, I need you to drop everything and pull what you have on the resort deal."

"Isn't that something your assistant could do?"

Since when did his employees second-guess him? Even if Roberto was right. Xander's back teeth ground together. He got Roberto's veiled message: Xander wasn't giving him tasks worthy of his position.

Xander's grip on the phone tightened. "Amara won't know what all needs pulled. Once you have the information gathered, give it to Amara. She'll see that I get it."

"Yes, sir."

"Thanks. I don't know when I'll be back. You can reach me on my cell if anything comes up."

"In the meantime, is there anything I can do?"

Xander had always been on top of everything. He didn't see a reason to change that now. Still, it wouldn't hurt to give Roberto a little more responsibility. After all, Roberto was a good man and quite capable. "Yes. Make sure nothing goes awry while I'm out of the office. We have a number of deals in the works. Are you up for the task?"

"I am." There was absolutely no hesitation in his voice.

"Keep me in the loop."

"Yes, sir."

They went over a couple of other open items and then he was transferred to his assistant. In addition to other tasks, he requested she send him clothes—casual clothes. He had no idea how long he'd remain on Infinity Island.

For the moment, Xander was free to focus solely on Lea and the baby. And his first order of business was to tell Lea that he would invest in her island, even though he didn't believe in what it stood for—infinite love. That kind of love didn't exist. But he'd keep that last part to himself.

"What do you mean Xander's here?"

Lea really didn't want to talk about this latest development in her personal life, but Popi wasn't about to let it go. Lea looked over the top of her computer monitor and took in her friend's pink top that said, "Precious Cargo Onboard." Popi had volunteered to be a surrogate for her sister and brother-in-law.

Before Lea answered her best friend's question, which inevitably would lead to another one, Lea had a question of her own. "Where did you get that top?"

Popi sent her a puzzled look before glancing down. "I ordered it online. And their stuff is so comfy I've ordered more."

"Do they have anything more professional? I hardly fit in any of my clothes." The truth was she didn't fit in them, at least not the way they were supposed to be worn.

Popi nodded and then gave her the web address. "Now, stop changing the subject."

"What were we discussing?" Lea knew perfectly well the topic of conversation, but she was amused when Popi became frustrated and pinched her lips together like she was doing right now.

"You were about to tell me what Xander's doing here?"

Lea sighed. "I told him about the baby. I had to. I couldn't live with myself if I kept it from him."

"You did the right thing. But I thought you said he wasn't a family man. You said he was all about the business and had no room in his life for kids."

"That's what he told me when he was here last time."

"So once he found out he was going to be a father, he changed his mind?"

Lea shrugged. "I don't know. I told him about the baby last night and today he's here. I don't know what he wants from me. Your guess is as good as mine. But he is acting rather strange."

"Strange how? He wants to marry you? He wants to take the baby away from you? He's moving in?"

"I told you I don't know." She seemed to be saying that a lot lately. "The only thing he has told me is that the island is slowly falling apart and I don't have the funds to fix it."

"Ah… So he's still after the land. He thinks he can force you into selling it to him now that you're pregnant."

Lea wanted to disagree with her—to tell her that

Xander wouldn't stoop so low. But could she really argue the point? It wasn't like he'd talked about much else, other than how the island wouldn't be able to sustain them.

Popi was about to say something else when the office door swung open. There stood Xander, looking more casual than she was used to seeing him. Though Lea's attention was zeroed in on Xander, she could feel Popi's gaze moving back and forth between the two of them.

"I've got something I need to do," Popi said hesitantly. "I'll, uh, just catch up with you later."

"Sounds good." Lea continued to stare at Xander as he stared right back at her, making her heart race.

She wondered if she should have introduced Popi and Xander, but it was already too late as her friend had rushed out the door as though the office was on fire. Besides, it didn't matter. It wasn't like Xander was on the island for a social call. Was Popi right? Had he come here because he thought he had a real chance to buy the island out from under her now that she was in a difficult position?

"You missed the ferry." She forced her gaze away from him and stared blindly down at her monitor. "The next one won't be here until tomorrow. But I can request a seaplane to pick you up."

"I won't be needing it."

That got her to lift her head. "You can't just stay

here indefinitely. Whatever needs said can be done via the phone."

"It's better face to face."

She didn't agree. Being so close to him distracted her. "There's no room available. And…" Her rapid thoughts tripped over each other. "And there's a wedding this weekend. And we're booked solid."

He stepped forward and made himself comfortable in one of the two chairs facing her desk. "I'll guess we'll be bunking together. Again."

Immediately her thoughts went back to the time when they had in fact bunked together, but there had been no sleeping done that night—no sleeping whatsoever. And not much the following night. Heat swirled in her chest and rushed up to her face. She immediately squelched the very steamy memories.

Stay focused. Don't let him rattle you.

"That isn't going to happen again." She maintained as firm a tone as she could muster.

A smile lifted the corners of his mouth. "That's a shame because it was quite an unforgettable night."

He's definitely right about that.

She gave herself a mental jerk. *Stay focused.*

She tilted her chin upward. "So, you see that leaving is the only option."

"Actually," he said, leaning back in the chair, resting his elbows on the arms and steepling his fingers, "you have an empty guest room. I'll just stay there. And then we can talk."

"There's nothing to talk about." *Liar. Liar.*

The look on his face said he didn't believe her. "Even you don't believe that."

She leaned back in her chair and crossed her arms. "Fine. We can talk now. You start."

"I've had a look around the island and it needs numerous repairs and updates to bring it back to its former glory, as I'm sure you know." He sighed. "I don't want to make this sound harsh, but if you're already struggling, how are you going to handle things when the baby comes?"

She lifted her chin ever so slightly. "I have a plan."

His eyes filled with interest. "Mind sharing the details?"

"Actually, I do mind." Anxious to wrap this up, she said, "Now if there's nothing else—"

"There is something else." He leaned forward. "I'm willing to invest in the island." She shook her head but he continued. "You can't afford to turn me down." And then he named a staggering sum of money.

She didn't know anyone that had that sort of wealth. The things she could do with it. The island would once again glow like a rare Mediterranean jewel. They'd be able to take on twice the number of weddings.

But in the end, she knew what her answer must

be. "No. This is my problem. I'll fix it on my own."
She stood. "I really do need to get back to work."

A distinct frown settled on his face. "Why are
you refusing my help?"

"Do you really need to ask?"

"Apparently I do."

It boiled down to one simple fact. "If it's your
money, you'll want to call the shots."

"And if I said the money came without strings—"

"I wouldn't believe you. We aren't talking about
a small sum of money." She noticed how he didn't
argue that point.

"And that's it? There's nothing I can do to
change your mind?"

"No." She opened an email and started to respond to it.

He turned and started for the door. His hand
rested on the handle when he turned back to her.
"This isn't over."

"I didn't think it was."

"I'll see you later at the bungalow."

When he was finally gone and the door was
closed, she took her first easy breath. Why was he
sticking around? She wanted to believe that it was
because of the chemistry arcing between them.
But she refused to let herself go there.

CHAPTER FIVE

THIS IS GOING to work.

Lea had told herself that all the next day. An older couple, Mr. and Mrs. Kostopoulos, flew in that morning. To Lea's surprise, they'd decided against being silent investors. Instead, they were entertaining the notion of buying the island to run as Lea's family had done for decades—bringing two hearts together for infinity.

Selling the island wasn't what Lea ultimately wanted. But she was running out of time and funds. If she could find a buyer that wanted the island as it was, it would be better than selling to a developer like Xander, who was only interested in making money and cared nothing about preserving her family's legacy.

After a comprehensive tour of the island, they stopped at the Hideaway Café to get refreshments. Lea was so nervous about this working out that her hands trembled ever so slightly as she held her iced decaf caramel latte, a Lea-suggested addition to the menu.

The three took their refreshments outside to sit at one of the tables shaded by umbrellas. She couldn't tell if the couple was still interested in purchasing the island or not. Their comments throughout the lengthy tour were mixed. Her impression was that they liked much of the island, but she noticed how they were quite hesitant about the amount of work that needed to be done to bring the island back to its glory days.

"I hope you enjoyed your tour," Lea said to get the conversation started.

"We did," Mrs. Kostopoulos said. "It's so beautiful here. You're lucky to have such an amazing home."

"Thank you." Lea turned her coffee cup around. "I think this is the most beautiful place on earth. That's why I want someone who loves it as much as I do to take it over."

"I understand." Mrs. Kostopoulos smiled. "If this were my home, I would want the same."

Was that a gentle way of letting her down? Lea's stomach twisted in a knot. She glanced at her coffee, but she had no desire to drink it.

"What my wife is trying to say is that we love the island, but with us nearing retirement age, there's more work here than we are up to doing. I know that's not what you want to hear, but I'm sure you'll find the right person for this place." Mr. Kostopoulos paused. "Unless you already have—"

"Hello, everyone." Xander's voice came from behind her.

What was he doing here? Lea stifled a sigh. Why should she worry? It wasn't like he could do any damage now. The Kostopouloses had already turned her down. But Xander didn't know that and she wasn't in the mood to enlighten him.

Everyone looked pleased.

Was this it? Had Lea found people to run the island just as she wanted?

Xander's chest tightened. If she had, then his chance of being close to her and the baby was slipping through his fingers. She wouldn't need anything from him and she could go anywhere in the world.

The thought of her moving far away didn't sit easy with him. It didn't sit well at all. He could only think of one desperate move to make—marry her.

As quickly as the thought came to him, he dismissed it. There had to be something he could do that was less drastic. He just couldn't think of what that might be at the moment. But he wasn't giving up. He wasn't a quitter—especially when the stakes were this high.

Xander shook hands with the Kostopouloses as introductions were made. And then as quickly as possible, he drew Lea aside.

"Why would you sell the island to them and not me?" he asked. "If it's the money, I will top what they're offering you."

Lea's expression didn't reveal her reaction. In

a calm voice, she said, "It isn't about the money. What the baby and I need can't be bought and paid for."

He studied her for a moment. Was she saying that she wanted a family? With him? Impossible. She'd already made it clear that she could get by on her own.

Still, he thought she was being foolish for clinging to her pride instead of taking the money. In his business, he hadn't met many people who didn't value money above most everything. But the better he got to know Lea, the more he realized she was unlike anyone else he'd ever known.

"I need to get back to my guests," she said.

As she began to turn away, he instinctively reached out to her. His hand skimmed down her forearm and caught hold of her hand. She turned back with a surprised look in her eyes that were more green than blue today.

And then her gaze lowered to their clasped hands. He reluctantly let go of her. He was surprised by how much he missed her touch.

"Lea, please reconsider."

"I don't want to be indebted to you." She shook her head. "It wouldn't work."

She walked away before he could figure out his next words.

He remained at the café and purchased a black coffee while Lea escorted the couple to the seaplane waiting in the marina. He wondered if she'd made the deal. He couldn't tell. From where he stood by the railing of the café that looked out over the cove, he was able to see them on the dock. Lea shook hands with the man and the woman gave her a hug. It was a very friendly exchange.

Xander's jaw tightened. He had to make some big decisions and quickly. The first being, how far was he willing to go for Lea and the baby? To his surprise, he didn't have to think very long. The truth was he'd known the answer all along. He'd do whatever it took to keep them in his life.

Trying to invest in the island wasn't working. It seemed like Lea would rather let it fall into complete and utter ruin rather than take his money. He supposed it was because she felt a protectiveness toward this place. He'd never felt that sort of connection to any place. His lack of connection was what had made it easy for him to buy properties and sell them without any hesitation. Even his parents' home hadn't been hard for him to sell after their deaths. His sister, on the other hand, had an awful time parting with it. And for her sake, he had let his sister set the pace of the sale.

But Lea hadn't grown up on the island. It wasn't steeped in childhood memories for her. And yet she seemed to have automatically bonded with the island.

However, the more time he spent here, the more

solace he found in its peacefulness. There was no rush-rush, no aggressive traffic with the angry horn blasts, and everyone was so friendly and helpful.

He needed a Plan B. That was how he'd gotten to the top of his professional world. So if he came at this from a business view, the first thing he needed to do was more research. He needed to learn how this island and Lea's business worked. It might just give him the insight he needed.

CHAPTER SIX

HIS GAZE FOLLOWED HER.

She could sense it.

It was late in the afternoon when Lea had finished with her guests. As she saw them off on a seaplane, she was aware Xander stood at the café, looking directly at her, but she turned her back and walked in the opposite direction.

She resisted the urge to glance over her shoulder. She'd made her decision and she wasn't going to change her mind now. It wouldn't work having Xander overseeing her every move and second-guessing her plans. He was used to being the one calling the shots and eventually he'd take over the operation of Infinity Island—just like Charles had attempted to take over her life.

Charles had been her boyfriend in college. At first, she'd thought it was cute how he would order for both of them at the restaurant. But then his opinion started to override hers in other areas of her life, from what movie to watch to what vehicle to buy. Eventually her voice was drowned out.

It took her roommate pointing this out for Lea to see what she'd let happen. And then she'd dumped him. He hadn't taken it well, telling her that she didn't know what she wanted—that she was allowing her friends to influence her. That last part would have made her laugh if he hadn't just done that very thing to her.

When Charles had pleaded with her to take him back, she'd given him the short answer. No. Unable to accept rejection, he'd persisted. She'd firmly held her ground. Eventually he'd gotten the message.

She had a voice and she wanted it to be heard. She had opinions and she wanted them to matter. She could make choices and she wanted people to respect them.

"Is this how it's going to be between us?" Xander's voice came from behind her.

She straightened her shoulders and turned. "I don't know what you mean. I'm simply doing my job."

He nodded toward the plane that was just beginning to lift into the air. "Did you have a good meeting?"

Lea hesitated, trying to decide how much to tell him. She finally sighed in resignation. "You might as well know that they didn't make an offer for the island."

"Really?" Genuine surprise echoed in his voice. "May I ask why?"

She turned to walk back to her office. She gave the hem of her blouse a firm tug, wishing it was a little larger. She'd placed an order from that online boutique that Popi had recommended and even with expedited shipping, it wouldn't get to the island fast enough. Sometimes living remotely had its disadvantages—but thankfully not many.

As Xander fell in step next to her, she said, "The island needs more work than they are willing to invest at their age."

"So they were planning to keep running the island as a wedding destination?"

Lea nodded. "That's the only way I would even consider selling the island."

"And so if I were to promise to keep the wedding business going just as you have it, you would sell to me?"

Lea stopped just outside her office and looked at him. "Do you even know what goes into running Infinity Island?"

"I guess not."

"That's what I figured." She opened the door and stepped inside.

Xander was right behind her. She could see why he was so successful as a businessman. He never gave up when he wanted something. But this time he wasn't going to get his way—no matter how much money he threw at her.

The breath hitched in her throat. Had she really thought that? Was she really that dedicated to her family's tradition that she would pass up a fortune in order to keep this island?

And the answer was a resounding yes. She loved the island. She loved the people that worked here. And she loved bringing two hearts together for all of infinity. The fact that there was no record of a couple married on the island ever getting a divorce was the most amazing thing about the place.

With so much chaos and hate in this world, finding a place full of love was rare. There was something magical about this island. It was worth fighting for.

"What are you thinking?" Xander's voice interrupted her thoughts.

"I was thinking how special this island is."

"Tell me about it."

She turned to him. "Like you want to learn about the wedding business."

"I do."

She shook her head. "You just want to figure out a way to level it and build your mansions."

"Lea—" he stepped closer until they were just inches apart "—I'm being serious. I realize that you're never going to allow me or anyone to develop this island. I've made peace with that. But I can't just walk away without understanding what goes on here—what makes it so special."

She studied him for a moment. "You're being on the level?"

"I am."

"You want to learn what? How I decide who

gets married here? And how we have a hundred percent success rate of picking the couples that will make it through all of infinity?"

He shrugged. "Yes. You have to realize that it sounds totally impossible. Couples just don't stay together for long these days. Divorce, well, it's the norm."

"Not in my world." If she got married, it would be forever. "If a couple is married here on the island, they stay married."

"Show me."

Lea moved behind her desk. "Show you what?"

"How it all works? I want to see this in action."

"But I can't. I don't have anyone right now applying to marry on the island. I've had to cut back on how many couples we can take."

He dropped down in a chair. "How does it start?"

He really was curious. She couldn't help but be a bit proud of her work on the island. And most people never bothered to find out more about what she actually did. What would it hurt to give him a little insight into the process? It wasn't like he was going to start his own wedding venue. The thought made her smile.

"What's so funny?" he asked.

"I was just thinking of you as a matchmaker."

He gave a firm shake of his head. "It's not going to happen. But that doesn't mean I'm not curious about your work."

"Come here." And then she typed the island's website address into her computer. "This is where everything begins."

"A website? Interesting. But I'm guessing your grandparents didn't have it so easy."

"No, they didn't. They would advertise in news-papers and magazines. Then they would send out questionnaires. It was a very long process. And it was still done that way until I took over."

"Really?" He rubbed his palm over his jaw. "I take it you've done a lot to speed up the process."

"I did…on my end. But it is still the same pro-cess for the prospective bride and groom. Digital or not, it still yields the same results."

"Mind if I try this process?"

He was joking, right? Why would he be inter-ested in a matchmaking program? But he was the first man to show a genuine interest in her work. And it felt good to be taken seriously. Her parents had told her coming to the island was a waste of her time—a waste of her education. The echo of their words still hurt.

And so Lea turned to her computer. "Here it is."

"Do you mind?" Xander indicated that he'd like to sit in her chair for a closer look.

"Not at all." She stood and moved aside, care-ful that they didn't bump into each other. It wasn't until now that she realized how little space there was behind her desk.

He took a seat and perused the home page. "I like the setup. For some reason, I was expecting a bunch of red and pink hearts everywhere and maybe a cupid or two."

Lea gazed over his shoulder at the computer monitor that displayed a photo of the cove at sunset. She'd always thought it was so romantic. If she were ever to get married, she would love for it to be on the patio of the café that overlooked the cove. She couldn't think of any better backdrop for a wedding. Surprisingly, none of her guests had requested such a wedding. Not that Lea was planning on getting married any time soon. She had other more pressing matters—like her baby. And saving her home.

"I don't run a cheesy business." And then realizing that she'd misspoken, she said, "Well, I do have a cheese business, thanks to the goats. What I mean is—"

"I know what you mean. I like what I've seen so far." He flipped to the next page. "The website is well laid out and contains some stunning photos of the island."

The web page also spoke of its history and how successful the marriages on the island had been. It also spoke of Lea's grandparents who ran the island before her. She'd come across photo albums with black-and-white photos. She was able to digitize some of them and include them on the website.

The next page contained testimonials of happily married couples, from people who were married just a few years to others who had been married fifty or more years. Talking to those couples and reading their testimonials of what Infinity Island meant to them was what drove Lea to fight the good fight. This would work out somehow. Infinity Island would go on being the stepping stone to happily-ever-afters.

The following web page was where engaged couples began their journey. Many applied to be married on the island but only a few made it through the process and were chosen.

Xander studied the page. "So this is it? They just fill out this form and you know whether they are lifelong partners or not?"

"Something like that." She wasn't about to give away her family's secret. There was a certain, some might call it, magic to it all.

"I don't know." Xander rubbed the back of his neck. "I just don't see how this survey or whatever you call it can pick out true love. I'm not even sure there is such a thing."

"Trust me, there is. I know. I've seen it." And though she was still upset with her parents, she knew they had found true love—even if they hadn't been married on the island.

"What's the matter?" Xander's voice drew her out of her thoughts.

"What?"

"You were frowning. Was it something I said?"

She shook her head. "It wasn't you."

"Then what's the matter? If it's something I can help with, I will."

Really? He wanted to help her? The thought of not being in this game called life all alone sounded nice. Sure, she had Popi, but right now her best friend was very distracted with the baby she was carrying for her sister and brother-in-law.

She shook her head. "It's nothing."

Xander sent her a look that said he didn't believe her, but he thankfully let the subject drop. "Can I take one of your surveys?"

"Why would you want to do that?" She arched a brow. "Are you planning to get married soon?"

"I'd like to learn more about your process."

She noticed how he ignored her question about him getting married soon. She wondered if she should read something into that...or not. Still, the thought of him being involved with someone sent a burning sensation in her stomach. She refused to let herself accept the reason for such a reaction.

"I don't know—"

"I just can't believe such innocent questions can predict a lifetime of happiness." He turned the chair around to face her, causing her to jump back. "Have you ever taken the survey?"

She shook her head. "I've never had a reason to."

"Not even out of curiosity to see how exactly it works?"

"Not even then."

"Well then, I want to take the survey. I'm curious to see what sort of results this mysterious and accurate system produces."

"But you can't." When frown lines bracketed his lips and eyes, she added, "I mean the system is geared for two people to take it. One person can't do it alone."

"Then you can take it with me."

She shook her head. "I don't think so."

"Is that because you know all of the right answers?"

"There are no right answers. It's a compatibility test."

"Then take it with me."

"But we already know that we're not compatible." And then her mind flashed back to that amazing weekend they'd spent together. For those few days, they'd been quite compatible.

"I'm not so sure about that. Why don't we take the test and see?"

He knew as well as she did that their weekend together was just a fluke. A momentary suspension of reality. There was no way they would ever get along that amazingly in real life. It had been an illusion—a moment of deep infatuation.

"I don't think so," she said, turning to the pile of mail on the side of her desk. "I still have a lot of work to do."

"I think you're afraid to take the survey with me." His eyes challenged her. "I think you're afraid of what the results will say."

She pressed her hands to her hips and stared at him. "I'm not afraid." When he continued to stare at her with a look of disbelief in his eyes, she said, "I'm not." And then with a dramatic sigh, for his sake, she said, "Fine. Let's get this over with. I really do have work to do."

A small smile of victory pulled at the corners of his mouth. Happiness was a good look on him. It eased his frown lines and made him look more handsome than any man had a right to.

She walked over to a cabinet where she kept some digital tablets that she used when working with the bride and groom as well as the wedding party. It was always so much easier to show people what she meant rather than explain everything.

She pulled up the website and then handed Xander one of the tablets. She kept the other one. She moved to one of the chairs opposite the desk. The added space between them made it easier for her to think clearly.

"I thought we were supposed to do this together," he said.

"We are." She stared at her tablet because every

time she stared into his eyes, it felt like a swarm of butterflies was set loose in her stomach. "I have both tablets set up so that we are on the same survey. Just follow the questions."

"Seriously?"

She glanced up to find him frowning at the tablet. "What's wrong now?"

"It wants to know my favorite color."

"And?"

"Well, that doesn't seem like a very definitive question. How is it going to decide if we're compatible by the color I choose?"

"That's the mystery of the survey. Don't think you're the first to try to figure out the inner workings of the system."

"Really? Others have tried to copy you?"

She nodded. "And not just since I took over the business but when my aunt was running it. I even found correspondence of people and companies trying to buy the information from my grandparents."

"And they always turned them down?"

She nodded. "Some things are worth more than money. And it's not just the survey. There's something special about Infinity Island. A number of the couples married here come back year after year for their anniversary."

"I must admit that I just don't get it, but I can't argue with the results you've been getting year after year, decade after decade."

"So what is it?" He looked confused, so she clarified. "What is your favorite color?"

"Isn't that cheating?"

"No. I don't have that question."

He shook his head as though he were utterly flummoxed. "It's red."

"Sounds about right." Red was a color of power—something Xander exuded.

"What does that mean?"

"Nothing. Do your survey. Remember this is your idea."

And so for the next half hour, they sat there in silence answering question after question about their likes, dislikes, personality and general topics. Lea had to admit that this was rather fun—even though she knew their results would turn out as incompatible.

"Finished," Xander said as though this had been a race.

Lea had one more question to answer. And boy, was it a tough one.

What do you like most about your partner?

Since all of the answers were multiple choice, she started going down through the answers. Eyes? Smile? Sense of humor? Voice? Kindness? Thoughtfulness? And the list went on.

Well, she did like his eyes. In fact, she could stare into them all night long.

And as she recalled, he did have a good sense of humor. He could even laugh at himself.

And there was his voice—his voice was so rich, like a fine dark chocolate.

How in the world was she supposed to settle on just one thing?

"Is there a problem?" Xander's voice cut through the debate in her head.

She clicked on the first option. His eyes. After all, weren't they the mirrors to one's soul? If so, there was a lot more to this man than she knew so far. And maybe it wasn't the wisest thing, but she was curious to know more about him. She tried to tell herself it was for the baby. When their child grew up, if Xander backed out of their lives, she'd be able to tell their son or daughter about their father. But she had a hard time swallowing that excuse. Her need to know came from a much deeper place.

"Finished." She looked up and found herself gazing into those eyes—the eyes that felt as though he could see through her thinly veiled excuses and the wall around her heart.

She glanced away. He couldn't see that much. She wouldn't let him.

Something was up.

Xander had noticed a difference in Lea since they started the survey. The questions of which he found unusual and sometimes quite probative. Like the one about what he liked best about Lea. That had been one of the easiest questions. He was drawn to her kindness.

Sure, she gave him a hard time, but that was because she perceived him as a threat—to her home, her independence and her ancestry. But he remembered the weekend they'd spent together. Once the business portion had concluded, she'd been sweet, kind and totally irresistible.

And he'd seen her with her employees. She was compassionate. She never asked them to do anything that she wasn't willing to do. He recalled her sopping up water in the honeymoon bungalow. She hadn't hesitated, not for a moment. She'd dived right in and gotten the messy job done.

Now if only he could get her to see him as someone other than the enemy. As much as he wanted to back away from this complicated situation, he couldn't. He believed her about the baby. Things had gotten a little out of hand that weekend and obviously mistakes had been made.

And now they had to come to an understanding that gave him peace of mind when he returned to Athens. He had no idea what the future would be like for any of them. It would help if Lea would tell him what she expected of him instead of being so stubbornly independent and insisting she could do everything on her own. They'd gotten into the awkward position together, and now they should both take part in an amicable solution.

"When will we get the results?" He had to admit he was rather curious to see what this survey would say about their prospects as a couple. He had a feeling it wouldn't be good. But that wouldn't stop him from attempting to keep his family together.

"Are you really that curious?" Lea asked.

He shrugged. He didn't want to reveal the extent of his interest. "I'm a businessman. I like to know how everything works—from a bystander aspect."

There was a part of him that wondered if Lea would accept it if this system—this reliable system—this age-old system—said that they were a good match. Would he?

Lea sighed as though in resignation. She got to her feet and moved around the desk, stopping next to him. "Do you mind?"

It took him a second, because he was so used to being the one behind the desk, to realize that he'd taken over her spot. He got to his feet and moved to the other side of the desk.

Lea took a seat and started typing on her keyboard. "Since I have automated the entire process, the results are basically instantaneous." She hesitated. Then glancing at him, she asked, "Are you sure you want the results?"

He got the feeling she didn't want them. Was

that because she thought they'd make a good match? Or because she knew they were ill-suited for each other?

Since he wasn't good with personal relationships, he didn't have a clue how this would pan out. And so he wanted the answers. He wasn't sure he would believe them, as he'd spent his life breaking through other people's expectations of him.

"Yes. I want the results."

"Okay." Lea paused and then pressed one button.

She gasped.

In a heartbeat he was in motion, rounding the desk to find out what was the matter. He stopped next to Lea's chair and hunched over to get a good look at the monitor. His gaze searched through the words, looking for what had shocked Lea.

Had it totally rejected them?

Was she worried about them not being suited to co-parent their child?

And then two-thirds of the way down the screen, he read: *Perfect Life Partners.*

"Really?" He just couldn't believe those were the results. Had Lea pressed the wrong button? Were these the results for some other couple?

Lea swung her chair around to face him, causing him to jump back out of the way. "You cheated."

"What?" Surely he hadn't heard her correctly. "I did not."

Her fine brows drew together in a formidable line. "You had to because these results aren't right."

He crossed his arms and stared directly at her. "And how would I have cheated? I still don't understand exactly how this all works."

She paused as though taking his words into consideration. "This can't be right." She turned back to her computer and started pressing buttons.

Xander would concede that they were perfect together when it came to chemistry. In fact, he would say their sexual compatibility was off the charts, but as far as being perfectly suited as lifelong partners—no way. Lea's system must have a bug. Because he was all about facts, balance spreadsheets and boardroom meetings. She was all about warmth, adorable animals and greeting card verses. Those two didn't sound like they were meant to intertwine.

"Well," he said, growing impatient, "did you fix it?"

Lea didn't move. She just sat there staring at the monitor. The same results were still on display: *Perfect Life Partners.* "There's nothing to fix."

He tried to process this. "So you're saying you and me—two very different people—are meant to be together?"

She didn't turn to face him this time. "No."

He breathed a little easier now. *Thank goodness.*

"It means that if we wanted to be together it would work—we would work." She swung around. Her gaze met his. "But neither of us wants that."

"Right." He didn't know if her last statement was a question or not, but he was agreeing with her. He didn't want there to be any miscommunication.

He may want Lea and the baby in his life, but it wasn't going to be some sweeping love story. It was going to be much more basic than that.

CHAPTER SEVEN

SHE WOULD NOT give up.

She refused.

Lea curled up on the couch that evening with her laptop. Since her attempt to find investors in the island had failed, she was continuing her search for someone already in the wedding business who was interested in spreading their wings. It needed to be someone that believed in love and happily-ever-after. They had to have money available to invest in something proven to work, that guaranteed one successful marriage after another.

Then Lea's thoughts turned to the results for her and Xander. Was this place and its methods so reliable? Or had they just gotten lucky so far?

She didn't understand their compatibility results. Someone just had to look at them to see they weren't meant for each other—not that either of them was even considering it.

Was it possible her family's long-standing system for sorting out the perfect couples was flawed? Had she made a mistake when she'd meticulously automated the process?

Yes, that was it. She must have made a mistake. She would have to painstakingly audit the entire process to find the glitch.

A fluttering sensation in her midsection distracted her. Was that the baby? She sat up straight, waiting for the sensation to return.

"Is something wrong?" Xander asked from where he was working on his laptop at the dining room table.

"I don't think so. Wait. There it is again."

"There's what?" A frown of concern pulled at his handsome face.

"I think it's the baby kicking." It was the most marvelous butterfly sort of sensation.

He knelt down beside her. "Does it hurt?"

"Not at all." She took his hands and placed them on her baby bump. "Feel it?"

He was quiet for a moment, as though concentrating. And then he shook his head.

She felt bad for him. "I'm sorry. As the baby grows, it'll get stronger and then you'll be able to feel it."

His hands were still touching her when their gazes locked. Her heart began pounding. It would be so easy to forget that they were only co-parents and not so much more.

Was that what she wanted from Xander? More than this one fleeting moment? If she leaned over and kissed him, would it be a mistake? Until she had the answer to those questions, it was best not to further complicate things—for both their sakes.

She leaned back on the couch. "I better get back to work."

"Don't you ever take time off?" He took a seat in the armchair just a few feet away.

"What kind of question is that?" She frowned at him. "You're a workaholic. I doubt you ever take time off. Your time on the island must be your first vacation in forever. Your work is the most important thing to you—above family—"

"Whoa." His eyebrows rose high on his forehead. "Since when have you become an expert on me?"

"I… I'm not." She inwardly groaned. She hadn't meant to let it slip that she'd read one, okay, maybe two or three press releases about him. "But don't all successful businessmen work all of the time?"

His eyes said that he didn't believe her flimsy excuse. "You've painted me to be some sort of villain, but you don't even know me. Not really."

The truth was she'd sought out every article she could find about him online. How could she not? He was the father of her baby. And so far, he'd been reluctant to share much about himself.

She crossed her arms. "Are you saying I'm wrong about you?"

He hesitated. "I'm saying you should give me a chance. Maybe I'll surprise you."

"You won't be here long enough to surprise me."

"Actually, I've decided to stay on for a few days, maybe a week."

"You *what*?" Surely she hadn't heard him correctly.

"I'm taking some time off from my business. You and I have lots to figure out."

Her lips pressed together in a firm line, holding back all of the reasons why his staying here with her was such a bad idea. And then she took in the resolute expression on his face. He was serious? He was staying? Here with her?

Unable to hold back any longer, Lea said, "This isn't going to work."

He sent her a reassuring smile. "Sure it is."

She shook her head. "No, it isn't. I have work to do. I can't just sit around and entertain you." She waved her hands around. "If you hadn't noticed, I have big problems here."

"If you'd let me, I could fix those problems."

If only she could trust him, she might entertain the idea. But she knew how much he wanted the island to add to his prestigious list of stunning properties. Besides, this was her problem, not his. She would figure a way out of it.

"I've got this." She hoped she sounded more confident than she felt.

Xander raised a questioning brow. "While you deal with those problems, I'm going to see about making the honeymoon bungalow usable again."

She couldn't believe her ears. He was volunteering to do manual labor…for her…for free. Impossible. "Thank you. But you don't have to—"

"I know I don't. I want to. My grandfather always said it was good to get back to your roots now and then, otherwise you're likely to lose your path in life."

This was a different side of Xander—much different than she'd known to this point.

Lea closed her laptop. "I do have someone who can do the work."

"And I also know you're understaffed. So let me take this off your plate."

It was silly to argue with him. She already knew he was going to do as he pleased, no matter what she said. And if he was busy, it would keep him out of her way while she continued her search for the perfect buyer.

What was it going to be like being Xander's roommate? Her gaze moved to his face and then lowered to his lips. She remembered just how good they felt against hers. She knew it was a one-time thing—not to be repeated. But that didn't stop part of her from wanting more.

It would take time.

But the important things were worth the wait.

Late the next afternoon, Xander slung a wrench back in the borrowed toolbox. While he'd done manual labor that day, his mind had wandered to Lea and the baby growing in her belly. He was drawn to them in a way that he'd never experienced before. It was like they all belonged together—though he had yet to figure out what that family dynamic would look like. There were so many details to take into consideration.

He picked up a few more tools that he'd used to replace the pipes under the bathroom sink. There shouldn't be any other leaks. He remembered how his father had taught him to work with his hands as a kid. His father believed in doing things around the house himself instead of calling for a handyman. However, try as Xander might, he never did things the way his father had wanted them done.

At the time, Xander didn't think he'd ever use what his father had taught him. As he'd disappointed his father time after time, Xander promised himself that one day he would amass a fortune and when he did, he wouldn't have time for such menial tasks. Xander knew that if he wanted his parents' approval, he would have to be extraordinary—

"Is something wrong?" Lea's voice drew him from his thoughts.

He turned to her. "Sorry. I didn't hear you."

"I didn't mean to sneak up on you. I knocked but you must not have heard me. What has you so distracted? Is it the plumbing? If so, I can figure out some way to get a professional in here—"

"Slow down." He saw the worry reflected in her eyes and rushed to alleviate her concern. "The faucet is all fixed and shouldn't leak again."

"Really?"

He nodded. "I replaced everything as the parts were pretty old."

He had a feeling the plumbing he'd just replaced was indicative of most of the things on the island. And if that was the case, Lea was in bigger trouble here than she knew. As his gaze moved to her slightly rounded midsection, he decided not to enlighten her about how extensive the repairs could be. She already had more than enough on her mind.

"Oh." She looked a bit flustered as though she didn't know what she should say next. "Thank you. You really didn't have to do all of that."

"I didn't mind. I told you I want to help you succeed."

Just then there was a flash of lightning quickly followed by a loud crack of thunder. Lea jumped when the bungalow shook. Xander's gaze moved to the window, noticing that it was dark as night outside.

With a hand pressed to her chest, Lea said, "That's why I stopped by. I wanted to warn you about the approaching storm. But it was moving faster than I thought."

Xander closed the toolbox and stood. He moved to the front door and stared out as big fat drops of rain started to pelt the ground. "Looks like we're stuck here for a bit."

When Lea didn't say anything, he turned to check on her. Her gaze didn't quite meet his. Ever since he'd surprised her by showing up on the island after learning he was going to be a father, there had been a wall between them. And he really wanted to get past it.

Another strike of lightning lit up the sky followed by a crack of thunder. At the same time, the power flickered and went out. A few seconds later, the lights came back on.

"It's been a while since we've had a bad storm," Lea said. She moved to sit on the couch. "With all of the lightning, we should wait out the storm in here. Normally I'd sit on the porch and listen to the rain. It's just so relaxing and I love the smell of rain."

"The smell of rain?"

She nodded. "It's a fresh scent, unlike any other."

Not wanting this peaceful moment to end, he moved to the couch, leaving a respectable distance between them. When the thunder once again rumbled through the room, Lea jumped. He wanted to reach out to her, but he resisted the urge.

"I take it you don't like storms," he said, struggling to make light conversation.

"Rain, yes. Storms, not so much."

He had a feeling there was more to her discomfort than she was saying. He wasn't sure if he should ask about it or not. But if they were ever going to break through this wall standing between them, they had to start taking some risks instead of politely dancing around each other.

"Did you have a bad experience with storms?"

She nodded as the sky lit up again. Rain beat off the roof and echoed through the bungalow. "It was a long time ago. I'm not sure why it still gets to me."

Bit by bit, he could feel the wall starting to come down. He had to keep the line of communication open. "What happened?"

She glanced at him. "You don't want to hear this."

"Sure, I do. If you're willing to tell me." He realized in that moment that he wanted to know anything and everything about Lea. She intrigued him more than anyone else in his life ever had. Right now, she could tell him the story of her life and he'd hang on every word.

She turned her gaze to the front door that stood open. Only a screen door stood between them and the outside. A cool breeze rushed in, sweeping over them. But neither of them made any motion to close the door.

She stared outside. "I was only nine at the time, but I recall it so clearly. My family, we lived just outside of Seattle. It was late at night and I was asleep in my bed until a loud crack of thunder woke me. Until that point, I'd always been drawn in by storms. I thought they were so amazing, so powerful and so beautiful with the way the lightning would slice through the dark sky."

"I have to admit that I like stormy nights."

"After I was awakened that night, I couldn't go back to sleep. I moved to my bedroom window and while sitting there I saw the brightest light I've ever seen. It lit up the entire yard just like it was daylight out. Lightning struck the huge tree near our house."

He hadn't been expecting that. No wonder storms put her on edge. But he remained quiet, letting her finish.

"The tree burst into flames. I didn't know what to do. I think I tried to scream but nothing came out. The boom of thunder woke my parents. Just as they got to my room, the tree split down the middle. And then one half fell into the house."

He couldn't even imagine what that must have been like for a scared little girl. He didn't move as he waited for her to finish her story.

Lea's voice grew soft. "The limbs broke through my windows, sending glass flying through the room. After that the memories are a bit of a blur.

I know my parents rushed me outside and a neighbor called the fire department. Luckily they were able to put the fire out before the whole house was damaged."

"And what about you? Were you hurt?"

"I had some cuts from the glass, but it could have been much worse. It's not like…"

And then she stopped. She was leaving something important out. They were finally getting somewhere. He willed her not to shut down now.

"It's not like what?" His tone was soft and coaxing.

"It's not like…like I was burned like my father." She glanced down at her hands that were clenched in her lap. "He was burned by a falling branch while he was trying to use the garden hose to put out the flames."

"That must have been horrible for all of you."

She nodded. "It was. My father's scars are a constant reminder of that night and how close we came to losing him. Every time I see his scars, I'm hit with a fresh wave of guilt."

"Why should you feel guilty?" Xander didn't understand. It was all due to Mother Nature and that was something no one could control.

"Because I was enthralled with the storm. I wished for more lightning. I'd willed it closer to my house so I could see it better."

At last he saw where she was going with this.

"And so you feel like you wished the harm on your father."

"In a way. And I guess that's why I let my parents manipulate me for so long." Her gaze didn't quite meet his. "But learning the depth of the secrets they'd kept from me ended all of that. You probably think I'm silly for letting it go on for so long."

"I don't think you're silly." He reached out to her, placing a finger beneath her chin. He guided her face around until their eyes met. "I think you're a very caring person, who loves her father very much. I'm sure he never would have blamed you, so you should stop blaming yourself for something you had no control over. If wishes could control the weather, I guarantee you that it wouldn't be storming on Infinity Island right now."

"I don't know why I told you all of that."

Their gazes connected. He noticed how her eyes were more green than blue. It didn't seem to matter what color they were. He found them captivating.

And then his gaze lowered to her lips. There was no lipstick on them. No gloss or any other makeup. It was just her pink flesh and he was taunted by the memory of her sweet kisses.

He swallowed hard. "Do you know how much I want to kiss you?"

When she didn't say a word nor did she pull

away, he took that to mean she wanted the same thing. He wondered if it could be as good as he remembered. He'd heard it said that you could make of your memories what you wanted. He'd been telling himself that he'd exaggerated the sweetness of her kiss because no kiss could be that good.

But when his lips pressed to hers, his heart pounded so loudly that it echoed in his ears. He'd never wanted something so much in his life. Her lips were soft and smooth. And in that moment, he regretted that they were seated on the couch. He wanted to pull her closer—much closer. He wanted every soft, curvy portion of her body pressed to his hard planes.

He slid closer until the length of his thigh was pressed to hers. The softest moan reached his ears as she opened her mouth to him. Their tongues danced together in the most provocative way. His hand moved until his fingers were combing through her silky hair.

His memory of their time together hadn't been an exaggeration. In fact, it wasn't as good as the real thing. Not even close.

And then there was the sound of a motor. He was certain it was someone passing by on the beach. He dismissed the distraction and turned his full attention to treasuring this moment with Lea. If anything was going to convince her that there were still unresolved issues between them, it was this—their undeniable chemistry. She had to feel it—

Thump. Thump.

Footsteps?

"Hello," a female voice called out.

Lea flew out of his arms as though the lightning had struck them. He regretted that their moment had ended so quickly. For just a second, he considered reaching out and pulling Lea back to him, but he knew by the serious look on her face that she would resist his attempt.

Knock. Knock.

"Lea, are you here?"

Lea smoothed her fingers over her hair before tracing her fingertips over her lips as though to hide any evidence of what had just transpired between them. But she was wasting her time. Her lips were now berry-red and her cheeks were flushed. She'd been well kissed and it showed.

He wasn't sure how he felt about her attempts to hide their kiss. He'd never been erased before. It didn't feel good. He wanted Lea to be proud to be with him. Not hiding this—whatever you wanted to call their relationship—from the people in her life.

"Popi, I'm right here." Lea started for the door.

Popi responded but Xander wasn't able to make out the words.

When his gaze turned toward the door, he realized the storm had quickly passed over. The sun was once again shining, but in the wake of the storm the breeze had cooled—unlike him. But the kiss would have to be put on the back burner for now.

Lea rushed out onto the porch. "I got caught in the storm and thought this would be a good place to ride it out."

Popi glanced inside. Xander remained on the couch. He waved at her. She raised a questioning brow before turning back to Lea.

"I see you had company."

'Um, yeah. Xander was working on the plumbing issue."

Lea moved the conversation to business. As she spoke of the upcoming wedding that weekend, he wondered if she had so easily dismissed that stirring kiss, because he hadn't been able to do that. Not even close.

But sitting here hoping she would return to him was pointless. He knew the moment had passed. And so he got to his feet and walked to the bathroom to gather his tools.

This thing between them wasn't finished. In fact, he was certain that it was just getting started.

CHAPTER EIGHT

EARLY THE NEXT morning, Lea decided not to rush to the office. After all, what was the point of being the boss if you couldn't give yourself permission to work from home. And so she quietly moved through the bungalow, trying not to wake up her houseguest.

She'd thought about having him stay elsewhere, but try as she might, the number of bungalows in good condition was quite limited and they had to be reserved for the incoming guests. She told herself that was the reason she kept Xander close by. She refused to acknowledge that she liked seeing him all the time.

As she settled at the kitchen island with her laptop, her thoughts strayed back to their time in the honeymoon bungalow. That kiss, it had stirred her to her very core. Her face warmed at the memory, even though she'd replayed that scene a million times by now.

She couldn't believe she'd opened up to him about her childhood. She'd never told anyone that story—not even Popi. It wasn't that it was a secret or anything, but rather she didn't like recalling that level of fear—so scared that no sound had come from her mouth.

By reliving that memory, she'd reminded herself of one other thing—she missed her parents. This long silence between them was taking its toll on her. She'd always been close to her parents until she learned that they'd lied to her about her extended family.

To this day, she still didn't understand their reason for keeping her from knowing her mother's side of the family. From everything she'd unearthed while here on the island and from talking to the couples that routinely returned to the island to celebrate their anniversaries, she'd learned her aunt and grandparents were amazing people. She really wished she'd been given a chance to get to know them.

"What has you so deep in thought?"

She turned her head to find Xander standing a few feet away, wearing low-slung navy boxers and a bare chest. It was all she could do to keep her mouth from hitting the floor. His ripped abs were better than the ones splashed across the sizzling romances she liked to indulge in late at night.

Then realizing she was ogling him, she lifted her gaze. When their eyes met, she found a big grin on his face. The heat in her chest rushed up her neck and settled in her cheeks.

"Find something you like?" he asked with amusement dancing in his dark eyes.

She immediately turned her attention back to

her laptop. She had absolutely no idea what she was about to type so she opened her email. She didn't care what she did right now so long as she didn't let her gaze stray back to his bare chest and those oh-so-tempting washboard abs. She stifled a groan.

"I thought I'd work at home this morning." The truth was her stomach was feeling a bit iffy. Her morning sickness hadn't been bad and had passed a few weeks ago. Could it be back? Or was it her nerves—between having Xander under the same roof and the dire straits of the island to worry about?

Regardless, she didn't want to go to the office only to make a spectacle of herself by running to the bathroom. But perhaps staying home wasn't her best move. "I'll just gather my things and get out of your way."

"No. Stay." His voice was so close.

He sat down next to her. She swallowed hard. She willed her body to move, but she remained there next to Xander as though he had some sort of magnetic force.

He glanced over at her computer. "Already working?"

"I have a lot to do."

"I see you have some emails about the island. I take it there's lots of interest in buying it."

Lea closed her laptop. "I'm still working on finding the right person to replace me."

"Replace you?" Xander was wide awake now. "I don't think that's possible. Besides, when we met you said you'd never walk away from the island."

"That was before."

"Before what?" He paused. "You mean before me?"

She shrugged. "A lot has changed since I met you. For one, I'm pregnant. For another, I've experienced just how much work this island needs and as you're quickly proving, it's more than I can do on my own."

"So you're just giving up? Walking away?"

"That's not what I said." But it felt like that was what she was doing. Her aunt had trusted her with their family's legacy and she'd failed.

"You can say it in some other words, if it makes you feel better, but it amounts to the same thing in my book. This is your dream. You shouldn't have to give up. There has to be another way."

"Sometimes dreams change." She thought of the baby. It was her priority now. Right or wrong, she had to do what she thought was best for the baby.

"I don't think you're going to be able to find anyone to take over the island and run it the way you do. You're so passionate about it—about bringing two hearts together. And from what I've heard, you're a terrific boss. Everyone on the island sings your praises."

They did? Her cheeks warmed. She was immensely touched. "I try my best. Sometimes I wing it. It isn't like this job comes with an instruction manual. But I'm sure there's someone who can do it better than me. After all, look around. This place needs some help—if I was so great, it would be all upgraded and fully maintained."

"You can't blame yourself for the problems that you inherited. These problems have been building over time. Some were covered up and hidden. But that can only be done for so long."

"It's just—" She was just about to say *too much*, but she stopped herself in time. "It's just time for me to move on."

"And what do you plan to do next?"

In that moment, she knew what she needed to do. Take a step back and reevaluate her life. "I'm moving to…" She wasn't sure where she wanted to move. "You know it really doesn't matter."

"Of course it matters. You and I, we're family now."

He stared at her for a moment. And she wondered what was going through his mind. Was he really worried that she'd disappear into the night? Or would he be relieved that she'd be gone—that he wouldn't have to deal with an unplanned family?

She looked into his eyes. Her heart started to beat faster. There was something special about him. When he looked at her, it was as though he could see straight through her—read her every thought—know the way he could make her body respond without even touching her.

She wanted to glance away—to keep him from knowing too much. But her pride kept her sitting there—staring at him. She swallowed hard. "Don't worry. I'll make sure you know where we end up." And then she decided to err on the side of caution. "If that's what you want."

"Of course, it's what I want. You and I, we have to learn to trust each other. How else are we going to raise a baby together?"

He had a point. But the "raise a baby together" part sent alarm bells ringing in her head. "How together are you planning for this co-parenting to be?"

This time it was Xander who looked uncomfortable with the direction of the conversation. At last, he said, "That's what we're trying to sort out, isn't it?"

Suddenly she felt as though she were on display—as though he was here to see if she was good enough to fit into his world. That didn't sit well with her. She didn't do casting calls and she didn't shrink herself to fit into someone else's mold. If she did, she would still be on speaking terms with her parents. The thought made the breath hitch in her throat.

Her parents, they didn't even know they were about to become grandparents. The thought of having a baby and not being able to share it with them made her sad. But how was she ever supposed to trust them again after they'd lied to her about something so monumental?

"How have your parents taken the news about the baby?" Xander's voice stirred her from her thoughts.

She gave him a searching look. How had he known that she was thinking of her parents? Could he really read her mind? Then realizing how ridiculous the thought was, she dismissed it as quickly as it had come to her.

"Why do you ask?"

"Because if you're leaving here, it seems likely that you'll move close to your family."

Perhaps she should have given her words more consideration before she dove into the subject of her moving. The memory of the angry words passed between her and her parents came flooding back. And so did the pain of loss when they'd told her she had to choose, them or the island.

Most people would think she was strange for feeling like she'd lost two of the most important people in her life even though they were still alive. But the people who had raised her—had loved her—had taught her to reach for the stars—well, they had disappeared somewhere along the way.

The parents she had now, she didn't know them. She didn't know these people that would lie to her time and time again. These people who stole her chance to get to know her extended family—her grandparents and aunt—they weren't the parents she'd loved. They were strangers to her.

And the people who had given her an ultimatum between choosing them or choosing Infinity Island—her birthright—had left her no choice. She wasn't going to choke down whatever lies they chose to tell her. She was going to learn about her family herself—

"Lea?" There was a note of concern in Xander's voice. "What's wrong?"

The backs of her eyes stung as the thought of all she'd lost came roaring back to her. She blinked away the tears. The last thing she wanted was for Xander to think she was weak.

She was strong—strong enough to raise this baby as a single mother. If he had any doubts about that, she would make sure to put them to rest before he left the island, which she hoped was soon.

She swallowed down her emotions. When she spoke, she hoped her voice didn't betray her emotional state. "My parents don't know about the baby."

His brows rose. "Why didn't you tell them?"

She glanced away. "Does it matter?"

His gaze narrowed. "What aren't you telling me?"

"Nothing."

"Oh, it's something. Talk to me. Maybe I can help."

She glanced at him. "Why would you want to do that?"

"Because whether you want to believe it or not, I want to be your friend."

"And not steal the island out from under me?" The hurt expression on his face made her regret her words. "I'm sorry. I didn't mean that." Not really. "It's just that everything in my life is changing at once and it has me uptight."

He didn't say anything for a moment as though considering her words. At last, he stuck out his hand. "How about we call a truce?"

She glanced down at his hand. The last thing she wanted to do in that moment was touch him. Every time their bodies connected, it was like her mind short-circuited. Still, he was trying to do the right thing. The least she could do was meet him halfway.

She reached out her hand and as their fingers and palms touched, a shiver of excitement coursed up her arm, settling in her chest. Was it just her imagination or did his fingers move ever so slowly over her palm? And there was this look in his eyes—the kind of look men gave her when she went onto the main island with Popi and they stopped in a *taverna*.

But then in a blink the look was gone, and after a quick shake, he withdrew his hand. Lea was left wondering if she was just seeing what she wanted to see or if Xander was actually still interested in her.

"There." He smiled. "Now can we act like friends instead of adversaries?"

"I didn't think I was being adversarial."

He sighed. "You're doing it again."

"Doing what?"

He smiled and shook his head. "So now that we're officially friends, talk to me. Why haven't you told your parents about the baby? Are they old-fashioned? Will they insist we get married?"

She leveled a serious stare at him. "You aren't going to leave this alone, are you?"

He shook his head. "Not a chance. I told you I'm your friend. I'm here to help."

Lea was surprised by how much she wanted to believe him. She'd been going it alone since she'd moved to Greece. She did have Popi, but ever since her friend had agreed to be a surrogate for her sister, Lea hadn't felt right about sharing too much of her problems. Popi had a lot to deal with.

Lea was so proud of her friend for doing something so selfless. Lea knew what it was to have a baby grow inside her and she didn't know if she could go through that very special relationship and then hand off the baby—even to a sibling. It took someone very strong, very loving and very special to be a surrogate.

Lea's gaze met Xander's. Sincerity and kindness reflected in his eyes. Maybe it was time she let go of the past and gave him a chance—a real chance. "My parents aren't particularly old-fashioned. I think they'd be okay with me being a single parent."

"Then what's stopping you?" He rubbed the back of his neck. "I don't know much, let me rephrase, I don't know anything about pregnant women, but I would think it's a time when a woman would want her mother."

She did want to talk to her mother and get her advice on different aspects of her pregnancy. Most of all she just wanted to share the joy.

"Under normal circumstances that would be the case," Lea said.

"But these aren't normal circumstances?"

Lea shook her head. She took a deep breath. If she was going to trust him, she had to continue opening up to him. "When I left Seattle and moved to Greece, there was a big blowup with my parents." She paused. How much should she say? After all, he was just being nice. He wouldn't want to hear the whole sordid story. "We haven't spoken since."

"I see." His expression changed as though he were troubleshooting the situation. "Maybe the baby could be the bridge to bring you back together."

Lea shook her head and placed a protective hand over her abdomen. "I won't use my baby that way. If my parents and I work this out, it'll be because they want to—not because it's the only way for them to get access to their only grandchild."

"You say if they want to, but what about you? Do you want to work things out?"

That wasn't an easy question to answer. "Yes. And no."

His brows rose. "Care to elaborate?"

She sighed. "My parents lied to me, both by omission and with flat-out lies. They didn't tell me about this island—about my grandparents and aunt. They knew if they told me I'd insist on coming here—on meeting and knowing my extended family." Just mentioning it made her body tense. "And now they are all dead and all I have are the pictures and notes that are here on the island to give me a clue what these people were like. It wasn't fair. My parents robbed me of a piece of my life—something I'll never get back."

"I had no idea. No wonder this island is so important to you. But surely your parents had a good reason to keep it all from you."

"According to them, my grandparents forbade them to marry and said if they did that they would disown my mother."

"Maybe that's why they didn't mention this part of the family. They had written your grandparents out of their lives."

"But what about my aunt? She didn't disown anyone. In the end, after my grandparents died, she was left on this island without any family. She was alone when she died. It wasn't how she wanted it."

"How do you know?"

"Because there was a letter to me in her will. She told me that over the years she'd tried to reach out to her sister, but the letters were always returned unopened. When the internet became a thing, she found out about me, but before she could contact me, the attorney told me that she died of cancer. Can you imagine dying all alone with no family?"

Xander reached out and pulled Lea close until her head rested on his strong shoulder. He didn't say anything. Instead he just sat there for a bit holding her until she had her emotions under control.

When Lea pulled back, she did so reluctantly. She hadn't allowed herself to remember how good it felt to be held in Xander's arms. And now as she leaned back on the barstool, she missed his warm and comforting touch.

"I should get to the office. I have a lot to do."

He nodded in understanding. "And I told Joseph that I would help him today with a bungalow on the other side of the island."

Joseph was a very loyal employee. He'd been working on the island for more than twenty years and he was a very talented man—a jack of all trades. But he wasn't a people person. He would rather keep to himself unless he knew you well.

"So you and Joseph hit it off?"

Xander nodded. "Is that a problem?"

"No. Not at all." She was just surprised. She wondered what Joseph saw in Xander to take him under his wing so quickly. "I'll see you this evening."

"We still have more to discuss."

As Lea let herself out the door, she reminded herself that the tender moment hadn't meant anything other than that Xander was a caring friend. She couldn't allow herself to read more into the moment—it'd only lead to more heartache for her. She knew that sooner or later the people closest to her would let her down.

If she allowed Xander into her life, she had to make sure to keep him at arm's length. That would prevent hurt feelings and misunderstandings. She told herself it was best for their baby. Two parents who could coexist in peace was worth the sacrifice of not finding out if there could be more with the man who made her heart race with just a look.

CHAPTER NINE

HE COULDN'T JUST let her walk out of his life.

Move to the other side of the world.

The following afternoon, Xander frowned as he entered Lea's empty office. Sure, he was rich and could travel, but he couldn't relocate his real estate conglomerate to the States. Nor could he afford to be gone for long stretches of time. And then what would happen? He'd have to choose between the empire he'd built and his child?

Could he do that? Could he choose between the two things that meant the world to him? His child? And his life's work?

It seemed as if it didn't matter which he chose. He would be losing a piece of himself. But he refused to give up. There had to be another solution—something he wasn't seeing—something within his power to resolve. Because he couldn't stand the thought of another man raising his child.

As the thought of someone else taking his place in his child's life took root, he realized that would mean another man would also play a significant role in Lea's life. Suddenly the image of a man holding and kissing Lea's tempting lips filled Xander's imagination. His body tensed as his hands balled up. That couldn't happen.

Maybe if he stuck around and showed her how good they could be together as friends—as business partners—she would change her mind about leaving. It would mean spending even more time here on Infinity Island. And that would mean complications with his business and his sister. Still, he had to make Lea and the baby his priority.

And with that thought in mind, he removed his phone from his pocket. His fingers moved rapidly over the screen as he wrote a message to his sister.

Unavoidably detained. The plans for the Italian resort will have to be put on hold. Sorry. Will make this up to you.

As though Stasia had been sitting there with her phone in her hands, waiting for him to send a text, his phone rang. Caller ID let him know that it was in fact his sister. He knew if he answered it wouldn't be a short conversation. Not by a long shot. So he let it go to voice mail.

The truth was he felt guilty and that was not something he felt often. He was used to making the tough decisions—the decisions others didn't agree with. But this time his decision was affecting someone he loved. It was a tough thing to swallow.

They both knew if he didn't fly to Italy the following week to close the important deal they would lose their initial investment and any future chance to take part in such a promising venture. But he would make sure his sister wasn't out any money—even if his own company took a significant financial hit.

It was only then that Xander realized he was gambling with his future for a woman who didn't even seem to want him around. That had never happened to him before. He was venturing into uncharted water without a life vest. And he was very likely to sink—

"Something on your mind?" Lea's voice interrupted his troubling thoughts.

He turned to her as she crossed her office to take a seat behind her desk. "Yes. I wanted to let you know that we've hit a bigger problem than was first suspected with the Seashell Bungalow. In this case there actually wasn't a leak with the plumbing."

"But the wall had all of that water damage."

"It's actually a leak in the roof."

"But the ceiling looked fine."

"The water bypassed the ceiling and made its way down the wall, causing problems with the wall and floor."

A frown pulled at Lea's face. "That sounds like an expensive problem to fix."

"Don't worry. I have this all under control."

She arched a brow. "You do roofing work, too?"

"No. But I know people that do and I've called in a few favors."

"Xander, no." She got to her feet. "You can't be doing that. This isn't your problem. And…"

"And what?"

She averted her gaze. "Nothing."

"It was definitely something. And what?"

Her gaze met his. "And I don't want to be indebted to you."

He could feel himself begin to sink and there wasn't a life vest anywhere in sight. She didn't want to be indebted to him, meaning she didn't want to be involved with him. The knowledge hit him with a sharp jab that left a piercing pain in his chest. If Lea let him into her life, it would be because she wanted to…not because she had to.

His parents had let him remain in their lives after his sister was born because they had to—because they were already obligated. Not because they loved him—not like they loved his sister. Growing up, he'd seen it was all about his sister this and his sister that. Even now the memories hurt, but he shoved aside those thoughts, refusing to get caught up in something that he couldn't change.

"You won't be." He said it with certainty.

She looked at him with skepticism reflected in her beautiful eyes. "Then why would you do it? Why put off getting back to your business?"

"Because you need help and I can help you." He sighed. "Lea, I know our relationship is complicated, but I'm not the enemy. I'm not here to pull off some elaborate scheme and steal your island away from you. I promise."

She didn't say anything for a moment, as though digesting his words—weighing them. He willed her with his eyes to believe him. He'd never had a problem getting a woman to believe him before—but Lea wasn't just any woman.

"If I was smart, I'd turn you down." She no longer looked upset. "But as my mother used to say, a beggar can't be choosy. And if you mean it about lending a hand, it just might help me land a buyer."

That wasn't exactly what he had in mind, but he could only deal with one problem at a time. For the moment, he had Lea's blessing to remain in her life. He didn't miss the enormity of the event. But he also realized that in order to keep Lea in his life, it was going to take more of a commitment from him than he'd originally planned on.

So he'd have to move this thing with Lea along—his plan would now have two parts. First, he would find a way to pay off her debts, as this island was special. It truly was starting to grow on him. And second, he needed to do something for the baby—something more than providing financial support. The thought churned in the back of his mind.

But he had to know exactly what he was up against. "How is the search for a buyer going?"

"I've actually had a number of inquiries. But none have panned out."

"Have you given more thought to contacting your parents?" Xander didn't want her to leave Greece—with each passing day he was certain it was a big possibility. It might be the only thing he was certain of at this moment.

"I... I haven't had a chance to speak with them. I've been so busy with the sale of the island."

"I see." But he didn't. Not really.

"What?"

He sent her an innocent look. "I didn't say anything."

"You didn't have to. You have that look on your face."

"What look?" He was a master at the poker face. It had played a large role in getting him to the top of his profession.

"The look that says you don't believe me."

"Why wouldn't I believe you? Or maybe I should ask why I shouldn't believe you?"

Lea turned to the window, keeping him from reading the emotions reflected in her expressive eyes. "I've been busy. I haven't had time to think about it."

So she was procrastinating. As much as he wanted to keep Lea in his life, he wanted her to have the support of a loving family—something he'd had a glimpse of when he was very young.

"You should call."

She turned to him with her arms crossed over her chest. "Aren't you being a bit bossy?"

He wasn't going to be distracted. "I mean it, Lea. Life is unpredictable. And it's short. Don't waste this time."

Her gaze changed. "You aren't talking about me anymore, are you?"

"Of course I am."

"I'm pretty certain you're not." She approached him and stared deep into his eyes. "What aren't you telling me?"

Xander rubbed the back of his neck. He hadn't wanted to get into this. For many years he'd pretended that his parents didn't exist. Which was a reason he'd avoided his sister for much of that time. She loved the memory of their parents and was forever touting their parents' merits. He never corrected his sister when she said how much their father loved him. It wouldn't have done a thing to make either of them feel better.

As such, he'd kept his distance from his sister until she lost her husband. Xander would have done anything to make her happy—even when she came up with this plan for them to go into business together. When Stasia threatened to go into the real estate market with or without him, he couldn't let her venture into uncharted water without him. He wouldn't let her lose her entire savings.

"Xander, talk to me." Lea's coaxing voice dragged him from his thoughts.

He shook his head, chasing away the memories. "You don't want to hear this."

"I do. If you'll tell me."

He glanced around the office, suddenly feeling boxed in. "Not here."

Without waiting to hear if she was going to accompany him, he headed for the door. The memories of his childhood came rushing back to him. He needed to get outside. He recalled how he'd constantly done things to get his parents' attention, especially his father's. When good things didn't garner words of praise, he'd turned to the bad things. Xander squeezed his eyes shut, trying to block the flashes of memories. Still, they kept coming. The good ones. And the bad ones.

He kept putting one foot in front of the other. He couldn't take a full breath. It wasn't until he was outside in the bright sunlight with the fresh sea air blowing in his face that his footsteps slowed. At last he could breathe easily.

And then there was a hand on his shoulder. "Xander, what's wrong?"

He shook his head. How did he allow this conversation to get turned around on him? "This conversation isn't about me. It's about you and your family."

"Talk to me about your family."

Why did she have to keep pushing this? He never talked about his family with anyone. *Not ever.* Unable to stand around while having his past dredged up, he continued walking until he reached the beach.

"You can keep walking, but you aren't going to lose me." She rushed to catch up with him. "You can't expect me to trust you—to open up to you— and you not do the same."

She was right, but that didn't make him feel better. He kept moving but his thoughts were light-years away, racing through the past. Lea wasn't going to understand. She was going to think, just like his sister, that he was making too much of things. His sister had never noticed how their parents treated their adopted child differently than their biological child. He didn't care what happened, but he would never make his son or daughter not feel good enough.

Suddenly there was a hand gripping his arm, pulling him to a stop. "Xander, are you serious about us becoming good friends?"

He stopped. He wanted them to be more than friends—he wanted the family that he'd been robbed of his whole life, the family he'd lost when his biological parents had left him on the hospital steps and his adopted parents had found he couldn't match up to their biological child.

But he couldn't rush things. He couldn't blink his eyes and create the perfect family. And he was beginning to realize this endeavor was going to require so much more of him than he'd ever considered investing. It would mean laying his tattered heart on the line.

He turned to Lea, catching the concern reflected in her eyes. "Yes, I want us to be closer."

She took his hand in his, surprising him. She drew him over to a large rock where they could sit and stare out at the sea.

When Lea spoke, her voice was soft and coaxing. "Tell me about your family."

His immediate reaction was to change the subject, but he knew this was his chance to gain her trust—to take their relationship to a new level. And more than that, maybe his story would convince her of the importance of clearing things up with her parents sooner rather than later.

"I was adopted." The words just came spilling out.

"I… I didn't know."

"I don't talk about it—normally." He struggled to figure out where to start. "I didn't know my biological mother…or father. I was left on the hospital steps when I was a few months old."

Lea squeezed his hand, letting him know she

was there for him. He took comfort in the simple gesture.

"My parents didn't think they could have children of their own and so they adopted me. For the early years, things were great. And then when I was four my mother got pregnant with my sister. Everyone was excited. Me included. But as my sister grew older, I noticed how they made time for her school programs but not mine. They gave my sister what she wanted but told me that I had to work for what I wanted."

"That must have been rough, but I'm sure they loved you, too."

"Really? Because I wasn't sure."

"Maybe it was just the difference of you being a boy and your sister being a girl."

He shook his head. "Don't go there. I've already tried to explain it to myself. But I know different."

"You know? You can't know."

"Oh, but I do. I had it directly from my father."

The painful words came rushing back to him. He hadn't thought of them in a very long time. In fact, he had told himself that if he didn't recall the memories for long enough they would disappear just like a nightmare eventually faded away. But as he recalled the incident, the exact words came rushing back to him.

Lea didn't say anything as though she was sitting there waiting for him to find the words to explain it to her. Why did he keep opening up more and more to her?

Xander swallowed past the lump in his throat. The best thing was to get this over with as quickly as possible. "I was sixteen at the time. I'd been getting into a lot of trouble at school and at home, while my sister could do no wrong. Now, don't get me wrong, I love my sister. She's great. But we are as different as night and day. She didn't have to fight for my parents' attention."

He searched his memory for that one poignant day that altered the course of his life. "I had just gotten my driver's license and I wanted my own motorcycle, but my father said if I wanted one, I had to earn it. I also had to pay my own insurance."

"Dare I say it sounds reasonable? You know, teaching a child responsibility."

"It would have been if the conversation had stopped there." He took comfort in having her fingers entangled with his. He rubbed his thumb over the back of her hand. Her skin was so smooth—so tempting.

"You don't have to tell me if it's too painful."

Those words were like a challenge to him. "I refused to accept my father's decision. I kept pushing."

"Didn't we all at that age?"

"It was during one of our arguments that my father reached his breaking point. He turned on me and said I wasn't his son." Xander had never admitted that to anyone, ever. Not even to his sister. "My father told me boarding school would put more structure in my life. That was when I told him that I hated him. I told him I never wanted to see him again. At which point he said unless I changed my attitude not to come home for the holidays." And then realizing he'd let the conversation get too serious, he said, "I bet you were the perfect daughter."

Lea was quiet for a moment. "Not exactly. There was this one bad boy in high school with a few tattoos and a big bad attitude that my parents wouldn't let me date. We did get into it about him, but looking back on it now and knowing the guy was picked up for breaking and entering, I'm glad I lost that argument."

Xander knew she was trying to make him feel better and he appreciated the effort. But there was more. He drew in an unsteady breath.

Xander raked his fingers through his hair. "Now that I'm older, I realize it wasn't all my parents' fault. I was stubborn and angry. Even though my mother tried to smooth things over at the holidays, I noticed my father never said a word. As such, I quit going home for the holidays. I either stayed at school or went on holiday with friends. During the summer, I would work for my grandfather— my mother's father. He was into real estate. He would give me odd jobs of mowing lawns, painting houses, and one summer he got me a job working with a contractor. I learned a lot that summer."

"What about your sister? She had to have missed you a lot."

"She did. She would call and beg me to come home. When I told her I couldn't because our father didn't want me around, she insisted on visiting my grandparents while I was there." Xander smiled as he remembered his sister's insistence that they not grow apart. "She was tenacious when she wanted something."

"And she loved her big brother."

He nodded. His sister's love was something that he never doubted. "She's great—even if she can be a bit pushy at times."

"You keep telling me that it's not too late to repair my relationship with my parents. Why don't you do the same?"

This was the part that hurt the most. The ache in his chest ebbed. "I can't do that—"

"Sure you can—"

"No, I can't. They died when I was in college. It was a car accident."

"I'm so sorry."

"My grandparents took in my sister. I pulled away—even from Stasia. I felt angry that I had been robbed of the chance to ever fix what had been broken between me and my parents. And I felt guilty that I'd ignored my mother's repeated pleadings for me to come home. I knew my father would be there and I didn't know what to say to him. And in the end, I don't think he knew what to say to me, either."

"I know I don't have to say this, but I'm going to anyways. Your parents loved you. Maybe they didn't always show you how they felt in the way you needed them to." She squeezed his hand. "But they did until the very end. And they knew you loved them, too."

He shook his head. He knew she meant well, but she didn't know the entire situation. She couldn't. She hadn't been there. But he wasn't going to argue with her. It wouldn't do either of them any good.

"Why did you tell me this?" she asked.

He pulled back a little in order to look directly at her. "You know why I told you."

"It was more than wanting to share. Were you trying to tell me how important it is for you to have a strong relationship with our child?"

How did she do it? How did she see through him so clearly?

"Yes, I suppose that was part of it. I can't—I won't let my child ever doubt my love for him or her."

A big smile lit up Lea's eyes and made her whole face glow. "You already love the baby?"

He hadn't thought about it before. Not in those terms. *Love* was a word that he avoided. Until now.

He lifted his gaze until he was staring into the greenish blue depths of Lea's eyes. It was there that he found caring and understanding instead of pity. He drew strength in her compassion.

He knew how risky it was to love someone. He knew they could betray him. They could cut him to the quick. And yet in that moment it was what he craved more than anything.

Xander continued to stare into Lea's eyes. "Yes, I do."

Lea's eyes shimmered with unshed tears. She blinked repeatedly. "I'm head over heels in love with the baby, too. I never knew I could love anyone this much."

"Enough to give up your dreams here?"

She nodded. "Yes, that much."

In that moment, he felt a tangible connection to Lea. It was such a strong feeling that he couldn't actually describe it, but it filled him with warmth.

With his free hand, he reached out to her and traced his finger down her silky-smooth cheek. "Do you know how amazing I find you?"

"You do?" Her voice was barely more than a whisper.

"I do." His gaze moved to her lips. They lacked any lipstick and yet they were still rosy pink and tempting. When his gaze lifted to meet hers, he caught the spark of interest in her eyes. It made him want her all the more.

"I'm going to kiss you," he said softly.

"And I'm wondering what's taking you so long."

He moved at the same time she did. Their lips met in the middle. He remembered when they'd kissed in the past. It had been full of discovery and curiosity. This time, though, his mouth moved over hers knowing what she liked.

They may have only spent a long weekend together a few months ago, but the memory of her kiss was tattooed upon his mind. Their kisses had gone on and on, partly from an unending desire and partly because he knew it would end soon and he wanted—no, he needed—to remember the way she felt in his arms and the way she tasted so sweet like ripe, red berries. But those memories were nothing compared to the real thing.

As his mouth moved over hers, coaxing her to open up to him, he realized just how much he'd missed this—missed her. He'd tried fighting it. He'd told himself it wasn't her but the human connection that he missed. He'd told himself that he'd worked too hard for too long. He needed to spend some time away from the office.

But now, as his fingers slid down over Lea's cheek to her neck, he knew he'd been lying to himself. He'd craved Lea all of these weeks and it had nothing to do with his workload or his lack of a social life. It had only to do with Lea and how much he'd missed her.

Her hands slipped up over his shoulders, up his neck. Her fingers combed through his hair as her nails scraped over his scalp, setting his nerve endings atingle. A moan swelled within the back of his throat. If they weren't here on the beach in the middle of the resort, he would definitely take things further.

Before things got totally out of control, he had to stop this madness. But he made no motion to pull away from her. He needed her more than he needed oxygen—

That thought jerked him out of the clouds and brought his feet back down to earth with a jolt. He pulled back from her. He couldn't lose his head. Because there was absolutely no way he was falling in love. None. He'd promised himself that he would never let himself become that vulnerable again.

"What's the matter?" Lea asked.

He shook his head and forced a smile to his lips. "Nothing. Nothing at all." And then his gaze met her confused look. "I... I need to get going. I have to get to the dock."

"What? But why?"

"Those men I have coming to work on the bungalow—" he checked the time "—should be here now."

"Oh. Okay." The look of disappointment on her face was unmistakable.

He longed to take her back in his arms and kiss away her unhappiness, but he stilled himself. To do that—to cave in to his desires—he'd give her the wrong idea. He'd give himself the wrong idea that this relationship was more than a convenience for co-parenting their child.

"I'll talk to you later." He turned and started to walk away. He should say something else, but what?

"I'll see you later," Lea called out.

He stopped and glanced back. "See you then."

Xander walked away feeling more confused than ever. And that was a state he wasn't familiar with. He was a planner, a decision maker. He didn't have time in his life for indecision—until Lea stepped into his life.

Ever since that first day when his gaze had settled on Lea, he'd known something was different about her. He hadn't been able to put it into words at the time. And even now, he couldn't describe the effect she had over him. And he wasn't eager to examine it too closely.

But he was even more determined to do something special for their baby. He worried about being there for the child emotionally with his own scarred past, but he could do something with his hands—something to show Lea that he cared.

CHAPTER TEN

WHAT IN THE world was that about?

It was the question Lea had been asking herself since she shared that kiss with Xander the previous afternoon. She kept telling herself she'd been trying to comfort him and it had just gone too far. But had it gone too far?

Wasn't that kiss what she'd been dreaming about night after night? Didn't she want him to hold her in his arms like he'd done not so long ago? The questions whirled round and round in her mind.

And then she'd waited around last evening hoping they'd have dinner together—a chance to straighten things out—but he hadn't shown up. She'd even resorted to texting him but he hadn't responded. When she'd gone to bed, he still hadn't returned.

And this morning when she'd awakened, she heard the front door banging shut. She glanced at the clock to see if she'd slept in, but she hadn't. He was up and gone with the sunrise. Was she avoiding her? Did he regret their kiss that much?

The thought of him not enjoying the kiss as much as she had sent an arrow of pain slicing into her chest. She assured herself that it was her pride being wounded and nothing more. It had to be:

she knew to be careful with her emotions because people let her down—even if they didn't mean to.

The much-anticipated arrival of maternity clothes—professional and casual—wasn't enough to gain her full attention. Not even the little black dress she'd spent too much money on had nudged her out of her subdued mood. She told herself she'd indulged on the dress so she'd have something to wear to oversee the weddings, but she wasn't that good a liar—she wanted to look good for Xander most of all.

Refusing to dwell on a man who was now avoiding her, she closed the box of maternity clothes and turned her attention back to the computer monitor. She had a handful of new offers to buy the island.

As she scanned the offers, thoughts of Xander came back to her. She recalled how their encounter had started. He'd been trying to talk her into contacting her parents. A part of her knew he was right. But another part of her was still trying to deal with their betrayal. How could she ever trust them again? But she didn't want to end up like him, with no chance to right what had gone wrong.

She reached out for the phone on her desk. Her hand hovered over the receiver, but she hesitated. What would she say? Should she apologize for leaving in such a huff? But was she sorry? She loved Infinity Island and the people who lived here. If she had to do it again, she'd still make the same choice.

As her hand settled on the phone, it rang. The buzz startled her. Was it possible that it was her family? Maybe they were thinking of each other at the same time.

Knowing it was a silly notion, Lea checked the caller ID. It was Xander. For the briefest second, her heart dipped.

With an ache in her chest, she answered the phone. "Hey, we've been missing each other."

"Lea, I need you to come home now."

And then the line went dead.

What was up with that? She stared at the phone. Was something wrong? Had Xander gotten hurt? The thought sent her heart into overdrive.

She quickly dialed his number. The phone rang. And rang. But he didn't answer. What was going on?

She raced out the door, shouting to her assistant that she'd be back later. Her assistant said something, but Lea didn't catch the words. She kept going. Her thoughts turned to Xander and his cryptic phone call. *Please let him be all right.*

Lea jumped in her golf cart and set off. For the first time, she realized that living halfway across the island was a problem when there was an emergency.

The more she thought of Xander and pictured

him in trouble, the harder she pressed on the accelerator. Everything would be all right. But what if it wasn't. She floored the accelerator, wishing it would go faster.

When the cart skidded to a stop in front of the bungalow, she jumped out. She raced up the steps and swung the door open. "Xander? Xander, where are you?"

And then he stepped out from the kitchen with a dish in his hands. "I'm right here."

Her gaze swept over him, checking for any injuries or blood, but he looked perfectly fit. Noticing her white apron slung around his neck, she glanced at the stove to see if something had caught fire, but all looked to be fine.

"What's the emergency?" she asked.

"What emergency?" He moved to the dining room and placed the covered dish on the table where there was already a bottle of wine, fresh flowers and a candle.

She was so confused. "When you called, you said I had to rush home. I thought something was wrong. I thought…" She stopped herself, not wanting to admit how worried she'd been when she thought something had happened to him. "I didn't know what to think when you hung up on me. And then you didn't answer when I called back."

"Sorry about that. I was worried that lunch was going to burn."

She stepped closer to the table, taking in the perfectly made up table. "You did all of this for me?"

He turned to her. "Yes. I did."

She suspected he was up to something. But what? He'd avoided her since their kiss and now he was cooking for her? And picking flowers?

Part of her wanted to go with the moment and just enjoy the gesture. But another part of her wanted to understand Xander's motives. Her mother had taught her that if something appeared to be too good to be true, then it most likely was.

Xander lifted the bottle of wine as though to open it and then paused. "What was I thinking? You can't have this." He started for the kitchen. "I'll get something else."

She followed him. "Xander, what are you up to?"

"Why do I have to be up to something?"

"Because..."

He removed some fruit punch and club soda from the fridge. "Because what?"

"Because after you kissed me yesterday, you've been avoiding me. And as sweet as lunch is, I have to wonder what changed your mind."

He approached her. "First, I haven't been avoiding you."

"It sure seems like it to me."

He shook his head. "Remember I brought in a

crew to work on the bungalow?" When she nodded, he continued. "I'd heard there was a big wedding this weekend and you might not have enough space. So I worked with the crew late into the night and this morning we finished up."

"You did?" Wow! A big smile pulled at her lips. She recalled that there was a lot of work to be done on the bungalow.

He returned the smile. "I thought it would please you."

"It does." Her natural instinct was to hug him for being so awesome, but she refrained, unsure it was the right thing to do under the circumstances. "Thank you. But you shouldn't have gone to all that trouble."

"You're welcome. And since I can't help you carry the baby, I'm trying to help in other ways."

This thoughtful side of Xander was not something she would have expected of the astute businessman she'd met a few months back. But during his stay on the island, she was getting to see a different side of him—a side she really liked.

And that made her wonder if he was also becoming more invested in the baby—if he was thinking of playing a more prominent role in its life. Lea hoped that was the case, but she knew a life-changing decision like that would take time to adjust to.

"Have you thought about the baby?" she asked.

"You know, whether you're hoping for a boy? Or a girl?"

He shook his head. "Honestly, either is fine by me. But a little girl that looked just like her mother would be nice."

"Or a stubborn little boy with those amazing brown eyes like his father's would be so adorable."

A smile pulled at Xander's lips. "I'm not as stubborn as the baby's mother."

"I don't know about that."

"When will you know if it's a boy or girl?"

"I guess any time now, but I was thinking of waiting to find out the sex." She wondered how Xander would feel about her decision.

"Till when?"

"The birth. That probably sounds old-fashioned but I really enjoy the not knowing—the possibilities. Is that strange?"

He shook his head. "It'll be a nice surprise at the end of this adventure. But what will you do about buying things for the baby?"

She shrugged. She honestly hadn't thought that far ahead. "I guess I'll stick with neutral colors like…like pastel purple and green."

He paused as though giving it some thought. "Sounds like a plan. Now I better get us some lunch before you have to return to the office."

Once the bubbly fruit punch was poured into their respective wine glasses, he sat across the small table from her. He glanced around the table and frowned.

"What's wrong?" she asked.

"I'm forgetting something." He snapped his fingers. "I know what it is."

He jumped to his feet and rushed to the kitchen. She couldn't help smiling. She'd never seen him work so hard to make her happy. What in the world was he up to?

Xander returned and lit the candle in the middle of the table. "There. Now we can eat."

She glanced down at the food in front of her. A salad, pasta with a giant meatball atop it and fresh bread. It looked delicious. And she was hungry. Her appetite was in overdrive now that she was pregnant.

They ate their salads in a peaceful quietness. When they started to eat the pasta, she noticed that the sauce had a different taste.

"Did you make this from scratch?" she asked.

"That depends."

"On what?"

"If you like it, I made it. If you don't, I had nothing to do with it."

She couldn't help but smile. This side of Xander was like the man she'd fallen for when they first met. She was beginning to think she'd imagined his lighter side, but this proved that there was a part of Xander that he kept hidden from others.

She took another bite. It was definitely good—very good. All the while, she could feel his gaze upon her. When she glanced up, he was just sitting there staring at her.

"What? Do I have sauce on my chin or something?" She immediately reached for her napkin and dabbed around her mouth.

"Your face is fine. I'm just waiting to hear the verdict about the food."

"Oh." Heat rushed to her face. And then she had to decide if she wanted to tease him a little longer or whether she wanted to put him out of his misery.

The fact he wanted to know—that he appeared to care so much about her opinion—moved her. Her own parents didn't seem to care what she thought. And it wasn't just her extended family that they had decided she didn't need to know about. There were also colleges that had accepted her but the letters had gone missing. It wasn't until after she'd settled on an in-state university that she found out about the other schools. Her parents had told her that they were just trying to help her. Now she wondered what other parts of her life they had tried to manipulate.

Xander's phone buzzed. He went to reach for it and then hesitated.

"If you need to get that, go ahead," Lea said.

He looked torn. "Are you sure you won't mind? It won't take long."

She shook her head. "I'll be fine."

Xander slipped outside to take the call, most likely about business. Over the time he'd spent with her, he'd received countless phone calls and even more text messages. Business in his world obviously wasn't relegated to the usual office hours. The interruptions came at all hours of the day and night. He was a workaholic.

Not that she could point her finger at him unless she was willing to point it at herself also. It was more than a job, it was more like a calling. It was doing what she loved—making people happy by making their dreams come true. They filled out the surveys and then between her and Popi, they made their dreams a reality. Some weddings were classic while others were quite imaginative. Regardless, it was a privilege to be responsible for someone's dreams.

"I'm sorry about that." Xander's voice drew her back to the present and this lovely meal.

"It's okay." But she secretly wished she ranked as the priority in his life.

"It sure doesn't look okay. I wouldn't have answered but there's a multi-million-dollar deal on the line. And I just need to keep a close eye on things. But enough about work. Let's finish eating." He glanced at her plate with half the food still remaining. "Listen if the food tastes bad, you don't have to eat it."

She shook her head. "That's not it. The food is amazing."

"You don't have to say that just to make me feel better."

"Trust me, I'm not. If you didn't already have a career buying and selling real estate, I'd tell you to go into the restaurant business. This is amazing."

"If it's so amazing why'd you stop eating?"

She twirled the pasta around the tines of the fork. "See? I'm eating. I wouldn't let something this good go to waste."

He studied her for a moment as though he could gauge the truth just by staring into her eyes. The breath hitched in her throat. She didn't know how insightful it was, but she did know that every time he stared at her her heart accelerated.

When she broke the intense stare, she found her gaze dipping to his lips. What she wouldn't do for another kiss—another chance to be held in his very strong arms. A sigh attempted to escape her lips, but she stifled it. She didn't need Xander reading her every thought.

"You're being serious?" he asked.

"Of course. Why don't you believe me?"

He shrugged. "I just don't have much experience cooking for other people."

"Feel free to cook for me any time." And then she set to work finishing the delicious meal before it grew cold.

When she glanced over at him, she found his plate still had most of the food on it. It was as though he'd done nothing more than move the food around his plate throughout the meal. And now he was staring off in the distance.

"Xander?"

His gaze met hers. "What did you say?"

"Is everything all right? You've hardly eaten anything."

He glanced down at his plate. "I guess I was just a little distracted."

He set to work cleaning off his plate. But he remained unusually quiet as though he had a lot on his mind. But she wasn't going to push him. She didn't want to ruin the newfound peace. She liked it—perhaps more than was safe.

A few days had passed since Xander had come up with his idea of how to impress Lea. And he hadn't wasted a minute of that time. If this idea didn't win her over, he wasn't sure what to try next, but he wasn't giving up—

"How's it going?"

The male voice drew Xander from his thoughts. He paused from hand-sanding the cradle. He turned to his new friend on the island. "Joseph, thank you for letting me use your workshop."

The island handyman nodded. "Just make sure you clean up when you're done."

"I will. Don't worry."

The older man grunted, attempting to sound grouchy, but Xander knew the man may be crusty on the outside but inside he had a heart of gold. Joseph reminded him a bit of his own grandfather. Neither wanted to let on that they were both big softies when it mattered.

Xander had been working on the cradle for days—cutting, gluing and sanding. He turned his attention back to rounding out a corner. Maintaining steady pressure, he worked with the grain. He wanted this cradle to be as smooth as he could make it. No mistakes or blemishes were acceptable. He wanted everything to be perfect for the baby.

Xander paused to give the piece a quick once-over. Just a bit more sanding and it would be time to secure the rockers to the bottom of the cradle. The thought of his baby sleeping in it drove him to work harder—striving for perfection. And when his phone buzzed with yet another message from the office, he put off answering it until later.

Nothing less than his best effort would do for his child. And his gut told him that it would come in handy because Lea wouldn't want the newborn to be far from her side.

Once the cradle was fully assembled, Xander pressed down on the foot, making sure it rocked smoothly. There couldn't be any jolts that would jar the baby from its nap.

He stifled a sigh. He was tired of referring to the baby as it. Anxiousness consumed him to know if it was going to be a boy or girl. But what should the name be? He knew Lea wouldn't need his input, but that didn't stop him from going through names in his head.

Basil? Hercules? Kosmos? But it could be a girl. Hmm… Calla? Nara—

"Xander?" Joseph's voice drew Xander from his thoughts. The older man sent him a strange look. "Did you fill Miss Lea in on your plans about the cradle?"

Xander shook his head. "I decided to surprise her."

"You think it's a good idea?"

He had thought it was, but now he was second-guessing himself. "I take it you don't."

Joseph sorted through his collection of tools as though looking for something specific. "Don't ask me. I'm single for a reason. Can't figure out women."

Xander turned away as a smile pulled at his lips. "That makes two of us."

At last, Joseph grasped a tool and turned around. Xander couldn't help but wonder if the man truly had trouble locating a specific tool or if he'd used it as an excuse to linger…and chat.

"Hey, Joseph, you've been on this island for a while, haven't you?"

The man nodded. "Sure have. I was born here. Never saw any reason to leave."

"Do you believe what they say? You know, about the magic of the island bringing hearts together for infinity?"

Joseph glanced down at the long-handled screwdriver. "Don't have any firsthand experience, but I've never seen or heard of any marriage that didn't last. And it's been a lot of years."

Xander guessed the man's age was somewhere in his seventies, by the deep lines etched upon his face and his snow-white hair. But Joseph moved with the agility of someone half his age.

Joseph arched a bushy white brow. "You thinking of testing the island's magic?"

Xander took a step back. "Me? Get married?" He shook his head vehemently. "Not going to happen."

"Uh-huh." The man's eyes said that he didn't believe him. Without another word, he turned and headed out the door.

Xander stared after him, refraining from shouting that he was never getting married. It was true. He wasn't going to marry Lea, or anyone else, for that matter. He was not marriage material.

However, he and Lea were coexisting peacefully. In fact, they were doing better than peacefully. He looked forward to dinner these days. It was no longer a hurried take-out sandwich or Chinese in a paper box.

These meals with Lea weren't rushed. He actually sat down and noticed what he was eating. And best of all was the beautiful company. Perhaps he shouldn't dismiss the thought of marriage too quickly. There were possibilities.

But…if he did marry Lea, it would solve a lot of problems for both of them. And who said that marriage had to be based on love? Friendship, preferably with benefits, and the shared goal of raising their child would be a strong foundation. But was he dreaming of the impossible?

CHAPTER ELEVEN

AT LAST IT was done.

The cradle hadn't turned out too bad, if he did say so himself.

Four days later, Xander waited until Lea headed off to the office where he knew that she would be busy all-day meeting with various members of the staff as they prepared for one of the biggest weddings of the year. This time a member of royalty was saying "I do." A prince from some small country that Xander had to admit he hadn't heard of before.

Lea was all excited about the event. From what Xander could gather, the marriage had been frowned upon by the royal family and so the couple had decided to run off to get married and had settled upon Infinity Island for their nuptials.

When Xander had asked if Lea was nervous about going against the royal family and hosting the wedding, she hadn't hesitated a bit when she said no. The couple had passed their compatibility test. When he asked if she would have turned down the prince if he'd have failed the test, he noticed how Lea avoided answering by changing the subject. It left him wondering what she really would have done. Did people really say no to a prince?

But then he'd had the thought that if the royal family had rejected the union, would anyone come to such a wedding? Xander recalled the look of amazement that had come over Lea's face, like he'd asked the dumbest question ever. It would appear that everyone but the immediate royal family wanted to be in attendance, including an army of paparazzi. It showed how little he knew about these matters.

So while Lea was off dealing with the last-minute details for the big event, he had the bungalow to himself. He'd retrieved the now finished cradle from Joseph's workshop and carried it to the room he'd been staying in. However, when he placed it in the room, he found it didn't fit in with the decor.

The room was done up in yellow and teal. It was an okay room, but not for a baby. And then the next step of his plan to win over Lea came to him. He would create a nursery for the baby. It would be his gift to his son or daughter. Even if he couldn't be the loving, doting parent his child deserved, he could do this for the wee one.

He grabbed his laptop and set to work. There was paint to be ordered. Curtains. Furniture. And toys. Definitely lots of toys. And he needed all of it shipped to the island ASAP.

This was going to be the best nursery. It would have all of the latest techno gadgets to make Lea's life easier and the child's life safer. And it would be a fun room—someplace that his child would want to spend time.

And then he looked at the corner of the room and the image of him with the baby in his arms came to mind. It was such a foreign concept as he'd never held a baby. And yet excitement and longing filled him at the thought of sitting in a rocker and holding his daughter or son.

That was what he needed, a rocker. The perfect rocker.

His gaze returned to the computer monitor, straying across the date at the bottom of the screen. Somewhere along the way, June had become July. In the course of the two weeks that he'd been on the island, he'd gone from multi-million-dollar real estate deals to buying building blocks and teddy bears. Xander spent the afternoon researching baby products and ordering everything with expedited shipping. He hadn't been this excited in a very, very long time.

Now what color would Lea prefer? Hmm...

Life passed in a blur.

Lea had so much on her plate. It was taking both her and Popi to pull off this royal wedding. The budget was endless and the wants were continuous. To say the wedding was over the top was no exaggeration.

The theme colors were white and purple. The

garden was resplendent with large white trees strategically placed throughout. Purple floodlights highlighted them. No area was left undecorated, including the brick walkway to the garden. Arches of twinkle lights and flowers adorned the guests' path.

Lea had to admit she liked the part the bride had insisted on: when the couple were pronounced husband and wife, an army of cannons would shoot white rose petals that would rain down upon the guests. For that reason, Lea had insisted the vows be separate from the reception. She didn't even want to think what it would be like cleaning up thousands of petals while guests were milling about.

No part of the wedding was ordinary. Every detail was extraordinary in one way or another. There were even white and purple orchids cascading from centerpieces suspended above the tables. And above the flowers was a network of white twinkle lights. The stars would get some help that evening.

And if that wasn't enough, the night would conclude with a spectacular fireworks display. The bride didn't know about it. This was a surprise that her groom had set up without her knowledge. Lea thought it was a wonderful way to wrap up such an amazing wedding.

"Have the pyrotechnics arrived?" Lea asked

Popi as her gaze skimmed down over the extensive checklist for the wedding.

"They arrived this morning. I met the crew down at the dock. And you'll never guess who I saw there."

Lea glanced up from her checklist. "Please tell me the soon-to-be princess hasn't arrived. We're not ready for her. Nothing is in place and we all know how nervous brides can be."

"Don't worry. I didn't spot a nervous bride, but I did see a Greek mogul receiving a rather large crate."

"A crate?" Lea frowned. What would Xander need that was that big? "What did he say it was?"

"That's the thing. I didn't have a chance to speak with him. I was drawn away by the pyrotechnics guy. He had a lot of specifications for where the fireworks could be stored."

Lea frowned. She honestly knew nothing about these things. This was her first fireworks send-off. "Wasn't the warehouse good enough?"

"Yes, it was. But he wanted to make sure it was guarded. He didn't want any young kids or old fools to get near the stuff. He's the cautious type and frankly I couldn't blame him. The prince ordered enough aerial mortars to light up the entire Mediterranean Sea."

"That much, huh?"

Popi nodded. "I don't think the prince and his

intended know how to do things in a small way. But anyway, I was just wondering if you and Xander had decided to make your arrangement more permanent."

"Not that I'm aware of." What was her roommate up to? He wasn't planning to stay forever or anything like that, was he? She would get to the bottom of it soon enough.

But as long as Xander was distracted she could immerse herself in the details of the wedding. Still there was a part of her that wanted to drop everything and rush home to see what he was planning. Surely he didn't think they could be roommates forever, did he?

It wasn't until hours later that Lea was able to head home. She was dragging her feet, by then. The ferry from the mainland that normally only made one trip daily had made three trips that day to accommodate the supplies needed for the royal wedding. Lea couldn't even imagine what the arrangements would entail if this wedding had the king and queen's blessing.

As it was, only a thousand guests—the prince and his intended's closest friends and family— would be attending the nuptials. The number was too large to accommodate on the island, and special arrangements were made to ferry the guests back to the mainland after the reception.

The plans kept circling around in Lea's mind as she took the golf cart back to her bungalow. Tomorrow the prince and his bride would arrive. Popi had opted to see to the royal couple's needs, which was fine with Lea. The couple wanted to be here in advance of the big day to "make sure" nothing went wrong. Somehow Lea couldn't help but think that they would be more of a hindrance to the preparations than a help, but who was she to argue when the prince was the one picking up the large tab for this elaborate affair, including a bonus for pulling it together on a moment's notice.

When Lea finally let herself through the door of the bungalow, it was dark inside. She frowned as she flipped on the light. Where was Xander?

And then she heard a muffled voice. She headed for his room. The door was closed but light shone at the bottom. He muttered something in a grouchy tone but she wasn't able to make out the words.

She raised her hand to knock but then hesitated, not sure she should disturb him. But then again, this was her home and he was her guest. She tightened her fist and rapped her knuckles on the door.

"Xander, is it all right if I come in?"

"Um…hang on."

Something crashed to the floor.

That was it. She was going to find out what was going on. She grasped the doorknob but found it locked. Really?

She knocked again. "Xander, is everything all right?"

There was a slight pause. "Yeah. It's fine."

It? What was the *it* he was referring to?

"Are you sure?"

"I'll be out in a minute. Just get comfortable. I have dinner warming in the oven."

Dinner? Her stomach rumbled its approval. It had been a very long time since lunch. As her stomach growled again, she realized that now, being pregnant, she couldn't let work be her main focus and neglect regular meals.

And that wasn't the only change this baby would bring to her life. She wondered just how big a role Xander would play in their lives. Would he want to have their child every other weekend? Or would he take a more distant role? The thought didn't please her. Their child deserved to have both an active mother and father. But would Xander agree?

Xander sighed.

Putting together baby furniture was more frustrating than he'd ever imagined. And the instructions might as well be written in a foreign language because he'd done what they'd said five times and he still didn't have the changing table fully assembled. If the furniture was this difficult, he didn't even want to imagine how daunting it must be to be a good parent.

It made him think of his parents. With distance and a better perspective, he was beginning to think that he'd been too hard on them. Sure, his father hadn't indulged him, but he knew his paternal grandfather hadn't been easy on his father. So his father had done what he knew.

So what did Xander know about being a father? Would he repeat his father's mistakes? Could he do it different? Should he even try?

The questions came one after the other, but the answers didn't come as easily. However, he couldn't stand around in his room searching for those elusive answers. He glanced around at the ripped-open boxes and the furniture partially assembled. Maybe he should have waited to start this project when he was fully awake.

He turned his back on the mess. He'd deal with it later. His hand grasped the doorknob, releasing the lock. He opened it cautiously just in case Lea was lingering in the hallway, but she'd decided to move on.

In the kitchen, he found her staring in the fridge. "Are you hungry?"

She jumped and then pressed a hand to her chest. She closed the fridge and turned to him. "You have no idea."

He arched a brow. "You are eating enough, aren't you?"

She nodded but then hesitated. "I just missed dinner."

"I don't know much about pregnancy but I do know you have to eat regularly for you and the baby."

"I know. I just got wrapped up in things." The guilty look on her face stole his heart. "It won't happen again."

That was all he needed to hear. He moved past her and opened the oven. With pot holders, he pulled out a casserole dish. "I hope it's good."

"It smells delightful. What is it?"

"It's something my mother used to make. At least, it's supposed to be similar. I didn't have the recipe so I called my sister and she gave it to me. I don't know if it's good—"

"Xander, relax." She smiled at him for rambling on. "What do you call it?"

"I don't know the actual name but it's lemony rice pilaf with chicken. My mother used to make it when I didn't feel good."

Lea continued to smile but she didn't say anything.

At last his curiosity got the best of him. "Why are you smiling?"

"I'm just happy that you found a good memory."

She was right. For so long, he'd focused on all the things that had gone wrong instead of the things in his past that had been good. Perhaps he needed a different perspective on the past.

Xander dished up the food and then joined Lea on the couch. It was far too late in the evening to worry about proper etiquette. If he were alone in his condo in Athens, he'd be eating his food in front of the television, catching the end of a European football game.

"What were you doing when I got home?" Lea asked after demolishing half the food on her plate.

"I was just working on some stuff." He wasn't about to tell her about the nursery until it looked more like a baby's room than a junk room.

"Would that stuff be what you had shipped in?"

His fork hovered in the air. "You saw that?"

"I didn't, but Popi noticed you had a large shipment and she thought you were moving in here permanently." Lea eyed him up. "Are you shipping all of your stuff here?"

He laughed. This bungalow wasn't even half the size of his condo. His things wouldn't fit. If he were to relocate to Infinity Island, he'd have to build them a whole new home. Not that he was planning to move here.

"What's so amusing?" Lea asked.

It was only then that he realized his thoughts had translated into a smile. "I just found it amusing that Popi was jumping to conclusions. You don't have to worry. All my possessions are still back in Athens."

"Then what was in the big box?"

She wasn't going to let this drop until he gave her a reasonable answer. "It was some work stuff that I need to sort out."

Lea hesitated and then she turned back to her food. "Sounds like they shipped you the whole office."

"Not even close. But don't worry. I promise to keep it all contained in my room." He knew she liked to keep her bungalow spotless. Even the dishes were promptly rinsed and loaded in the dishwasher.

"Thank you. I appreciate it."

And then worried she might decide to start snooping, he added, "Just so you know, all of the stuff is confidential."

"Top secret, huh?" She sent him a teasing smile.

"Something like that."

"Don't worry. As long as you keep it out of sight, I won't bother anything. Not that I'll have any time, with the upcoming wedding."

And so he was safe for now. As Lea started to tell him about the latest developments with the royal wedding, he found himself interested in what she had to say. It wasn't the subject so much as the way she described things. She was an entertaining storyteller. He could listen to her for hours.

CHAPTER TWELVE

THINGS WERE GOING WELL.

Better than he'd ever imagined.

Xander surprised himself with how much he enjoyed spending time with Lea. He looked forward to their conversations. He even took pleasure in the companionable silence.

And for the first time, he realized his interest in Lea went deeper than co-parenting. There was something special about this woman that attracted him. Dare he admit that he could envision sharing his life with her—with their child?

It wouldn't be a marriage created out of greeting-card platitudes and Valentine's Day chocolates. It would be better. It would be based on mutual respect, friendship and attraction.

She wasn't as immune to him as she wanted both of them to believe. He noticed how she stared at him when she didn't think he was paying attention. And he saw how she trembled with desire when he held her in his arms.

But it was more than the undeniable passion they shared. It was something much deeper. It was her compassion when he told her about his parents. She hadn't looked at him with disbelief that after all this time he still cared about what his parents had thought of him. And she didn't look at him with sympathy that made him want to turn away.

She'd looked at him with warmth and understanding. And her touch had given him the comfort and strength to put words to the feelings that he'd been stifling inside him all this time.

The following evening, once the dinner dishes had been cleared, Xander turned to Lea. "Do you have any plans for the evening?"

"Just some computer work and answering some emails. Why?"

He stepped up to her and held out his hand. "Come with me."

She glanced at his outstretched hand and hesitated. Then her confused gaze rose to meet his gaze. "Where are we going?"

"I have a surprise planned."

"A surprise?"

He nodded. It was then that she placed her hand in his and they headed for the door. During his stay on the island, he'd made many friends. And one of those friends just happened to run the marina and had offered to lend him a boat.

Xander led her to the pier.

"What are we doing here?" Lea sent him a puzzled look.

"You'll see."

"Xander?"

"Trust me."

He climbed aboard the speedboat and then turned to her and held out his hand. She smiled. "How did you manage this?"

"I have friends."

"Friends, huh?" Without needing his assistance, she climbed aboard. "I think I'm going to have a staff meeting about not letting people sweet-talk them into doing things that are against the rules."

"You wouldn't get Caesar in trouble, would you? After all, he lent me the boat for the evening because he knew it was for you."

Her eyes widened. "So what you're saying is that you took advantage of our relationship to coerce my employee to break the rules and lend you this boat?"

Xander saw the twinkle of mischief in her eyes. She was having fun with this. And who was he to ruin her enjoyment? "That sounds about right."

"Xander Marinakos, has anyone ever told you how bad you are?"

He grinned at her. "And you don't even know the half of it. But I'd be willing to show you."

Just then he took her in his arms. His intent was to kiss her until she couldn't think straight—until the word "no" was the very last thing on her mind. But he also saw the surprise in her widened eyes as her hands landed on his chest. He realized he was overstepping their newfound friendship. And as much as he wanted to kiss her, he couldn't risk losing the easiness that had grown between them.

With great reluctance, he released her. If they were to kiss again, she would have to make the first move. He just hoped she didn't wait too long.

He turned his attention to the controls of the boat. "I thought we'd take an evening ride around the island."

"It's been a while since I was out on a boat. I'm afraid I've become a workaholic and spend most of my time in my office or else putting out fires around the island."

"Sit down, then." He gestured to the white seat next to his. "And we'll have a relaxing evening ride. I'm really anxious to see all of the island."

She sat down beside him. "Well, since you went to the trouble to get this boat, let's make this happen."

"Your wish is my command."

As he maneuvered the boat out of the marina, he was surprised by how true those words were. He was anxious to make Lea happy. Because when she was happy, he found himself happy too. And that most definitely would be good for their baby.

The evening sun sank low in the sky, sending rays of sunshine dancing upon the gentle swells of water. And as beautiful as the setting was, Lea found the boat captain to be even more captivating.

Xander looked at ease behind the controls of this expensive boat, normally reserved for the newly-weds. She was both surprised and impressed with the evening that Xander had planned. But a niggling thought kept intruding on her enjoyment—what was his end game?

"Something wrong?" Xander slowed the boat so they didn't have to yell over the roar of the engine.

"Um, no." She flashed him a bright smile as proof.

He gave her a hesitant look but then let the subject drop. "This island is amazing. It has so many different types of landscapes, from the smooth, white sandy beaches over by the marina to the high and jagged cliffs on this side of the island. This looks like a great area to hike."

"You're an outdoors man?" Somehow she didn't imagine him as one.

"I was when I was younger, but as the years have gone by and my business has grown, I've had less time for recreation."

"That's too bad. You know what they say—all work and no play makes Xander a dull boy."

He arched a brow as he glanced over at her. "So that's what you think of me? You think I'm dull and boring?"

Oops! Heat rushed to her face. "That's not what I meant. I… I just meant that you work too hard."

"And I'm boring."

"No, you're not." Her mind was racing to come up with something—anything—that would get her out of this awkward conversation. After this, she just might gag herself to keep from sticking her medium-sized flip-flop in her mouth. "Really. I mean it."

He flashed her a smile. "Relax. I was just teasing you."

She took her first easy breath. "That wasn't funny."

Xander stopped the boat. "Listen, I'm sorry. It's just that everything between us is so complicated. And I wanted to lighten the mood. I'm sorry it didn't come across that way."

She shook her head. If he was going to be open and honest with her, she owed it to him to do the same thing. "It's not you. I think I'm just a little touchy. I... I want..."

Xander moved closer to her. When he spoke, his voice came out deeper and softer than normal. "What do you want?"

She found herself staring deep into his eyes. Her heart pounded in her chest as the truth struggled to free itself. She wanted him. And that scared her more than when she'd left the only home she'd ever known to move halfway around the world to Greece. And it scared her more than the prospect of being a single parent.

"Lea?" His gaze searched hers.

Not trusting her voice or the words that might escape, she lifted up on her tiptoes and pressed her lips to his. She hadn't given it much thought. But he had asked what she wanted. And this was it...

Her lips moved over his. At first, he hesitated. It was as though he was surprised by her actions. This surely couldn't be that much of a jump for him. After all, he'd almost kissed her back at the dock.

And then his arms wrapped around her waist, pulling her to him. Her hands landed on his firm chest and then slid up over his broad shoulders. As he responded to her, a moan swelled in the back of her throat.

It didn't get any better than this. The setting sun in the background, the lapping of the water on the side of the boat and no one else around. Suddenly the reasons she'd been holding herself back from him didn't seem so important. Maybe she'd been trying too hard to keep him at arm's length. Because being in his arms was so much better.

Sputter. Sputter.

Silence.

Xander pulled back. "The engine died. I better check it."

With great reluctance, Lea loosened her hold on him. "What do you think it is?"

"It probably just stalled." He turned the key.

Sputter. Silence.

He tried again.

Silence.

"What is it? What's the matter?" Suddenly their perfect romantic spot seemed rather dark and desolate.

"Give me a second." He removed his phone from his pocket and turned on the flashlight function. He moved it around the control panel. "I checked the fuel before we left. It says there's still enough in there to get us back to the marina."

"I'll call for help." Lea dialed the marina office, hoping someone was still there. But the phone didn't ring. "There's no signal out here."

Xander glanced around. "It looks like I took too long circling the island. I don't think there's any civilization on this side."

"There isn't." Even though it was a small island, there were still parts that weren't developed. And this happened to be one of those areas.

"We aren't that far from shore. How are your swimming skills?"

Her mouth opened but nothing came out. By now, the sun had sunk below the horizon, sending long shadows over the land. And she had a choice to make. Staying here with Xander for the evening with the moon and stars overhead. The idea so appealed to her.

Or she could fess up about the emergency radio.

"Lea, it's okay if you can't swim. We can make do here on the boat."

"I… I can swim—"

In that moment, Xander yanked off his shirt, revealing his muscled chest. Any other words stuck in the back of her throat. My goodness, he was so sexy. Her mouth grew dry as she took in the spectacular view. She really was leaning toward forgetting about the emergency radio.

She kept staring at his defined chest and his sculpted abs. Her fingers tingled with the desire to reach out and trace the lines of his muscles. He was oh, so tempting.

"See something you like?" His teasing smile lit up his face.

Heat rushed up her neck and set her cheeks ablaze. The look in his eyes tempted her to start something—something that would most definitely spin out of control. But would she just get burned in the end?

The question had her hesitating. Why was she making such a big deal about this now? They'd already spent an amazing weekend together, wrapped in each other's arms. How could another romantic evening make things worse?

But things had changed dramatically since that unforgettable weekend. With a baby on the way, they would be in each other's lives forever and the thought of making that relationship even more complicated was the only thing holding Lea back from rushing into his arms.

"Or—" Xander's voice drew her attention "—I can go alone. I'll send help."

Evening had settled over them. But it wasn't that dark out, with the full moon reflecting off the water. She knew what she wanted, but did she have the courage to follow her heart?

As though Xander could sense her indecision, he stepped up to her. "Lea, it's okay. I'm sorry this happened. I swear I didn't plan it."

"It's not that." Her insides shivered with nervous energy. For so long, she had been enforcing the rules, walking the straight line, and now she was considering living on the edge and following her desires. "Let's go for it."

The look of surprise lit up Xander's eye. "Are you serious?"

She nodded. "I am."

This time she was the one to pull off her shirt and toss it on the white leather seat next to Xander's discarded shirt. When she glanced up, she caught him staring at her with his eyes rounded and his mouth gaping.

"What?" She refused to blush. They were both adults here. Consenting adults. "You surely didn't think I was going to swim with all of my clothes on, did you?"

And besides, her bra covered more than her

itty-bitty bikini. She didn't tell him that. But she couldn't resist glancing up at him as she shimmied out of her capris and stood there in her lacey boy-shorts undies. She heard a distinct hiss of breath from him. Playing the seductress was new for her and she was finding that she liked it.

"Last one to shore has to collect the firewood." And with that she dove into the water. She didn't look back as she planned to win this race.

The water, though warm as far as large bodies of water went, was still cold against her heated skin. She kept moving quickly through the water. The faster she moved, the warmer she got. And before she knew it, the water grew shallow and she stood up.

She glanced back to find Xander hot on her heels. She ran out of the water and didn't stop until she was standing on dry sand.

She turned back to the water where Xander was getting to his feet. The moonlight caught upon a bag in Xander's hand. What was that man up to now?

Guilt niggled at her conscience. She should have told him about the emergency radio. Just then a breeze whished past her body, leaving a trail of goose bumps over her skin. She shivered. She was beginning to think she was never going to get warm again.

Xander turned and retrieved the bag from the

sand. "I don't know if this is still dry." He struggled with the knot in the bag. After a few seconds, he opened it.

He withdrew a large towel and draped it around her. "I thought you might want this."

"Thank you. But what about you?"

"Don't worry." Xander wrapped his arms around her. "I know how to stay warm. I'll just hold this very hot woman in my arms."

"I don't know about being hot. I feel more like a very cold fish."

He tightened his hold on her, rubbing his hands over her back. "Definitely not fishy. I'm beginning to think you're part mermaid."

She lifted her chin so that their gazes met. "I take it you have a thing for mermaids."

"I didn't before, but with a little encouragement, I might change my mind."

"Mm… And what sort of encouragement do you have in mind?" She snuggled closer to him, seeking the warmth of his body.

He lowered his head toward hers. "This kind."

She tilted her chin upward. And then Xander pressed his mouth against hers. His lips were smooth and gentle. His touch sent an arrow of arousal through her core. Her insides immediately heated, warming her from the inside out.

And then all too soon, he pulled back. "I better

get a fire started. It might be a little while until they get here."

"Get here?"

"Yes, you surely didn't think we were stranded out here, did you?"

"So you found the emergency radio?"

With the moonlight highlighting Xander's handsome face, he arched a brow and smiled at her. "Were you holding out on me?"

"I, uh… Well, I uh…"

Xander laughed, a deep rich tone that wrapped around her and let her know everything was going to be all right.

He sobered up. "It's all right. I wanted to spend more time with you, too. But I didn't think you'd want to spend the whole night on the beach and so I used the radio to call the marina office. They're sending out a couple of boats."

"Well, aren't you my hero?"

"I'm just trying to watch out for a gorgeous mermaid."

A hint of a smile eased the lines on his face. In the dark, it was difficult to read the look in his eyes, but she'd guess that she'd stroked his ego enough to make him happy.

"Um, let's get that fire started."

"You might not find much to make a fire," she said.

"You know where we are?"

She nodded. "This is called Deadman's Bay."

He glanced around. "It doesn't look that bad."

She couldn't help but smile. "In the daylight, it's actually quite lovely with white sand and the aqua blue water."

"Then why such a dreadful name?"

"It's said that in the old days pirates would trap merchant ships in the bay and there was no other way out than past the pirates." She pointed in front of them. "The cliffs go straight up some three hundred meters or more. Climbing them without the proper equipment is a fool's mission."

"Well, then, before the pirates get us, I should search for some driftwood or anything that will burn." He headed off.

In no time, he had started a fire with the aid of a lighter from the plastic sack. She wondered what else he had stashed in that bag. Some s'mores would be great about now. Her stomach rumbled its approval. She wondered if they made s'mores in Greece.

Xander dragged a large log over near the fire and they sat down. He wrapped a hand over her shoulders and pulled her close. "Are you warm enough?"

"I'm getting there." Suddenly she felt foolish for stripping down and diving in the water. "What are people going to say when they find us sitting here in our underwear?"

"I'm thinking the guys are going to be very jealous of me being here alone with you."

"But…but nothing happened."

He leaned in close and lowered his voice. "Would you like something to happen?"

The word *yes* hovered on her lips, but she bit it back. Perhaps she'd been daring enough for one evening. "I think this is, um, good. You never know when they're going to find us."

"Really? Because I'd be willing to risk it, if you are."

She turned to look at him and realized that was a mistake. He was so close that their lips were just an inch apart. Her heart tap-tapped in her chest. She tried to tell herself that it was just the coldness but the truth was between the fire, the oversized towel and being snuggled against Xander, she wasn't cold any longer.

Her gaze lowered to his lips and then she quickly turned away before she gave in to her desires. She was marooned on this deserted beach with literally the man of her dreams, and she was holding back. Popi would tell her she was being silly. That she should go with the moment and enjoy it—enjoy him. But Lea had a baby to think about. She couldn't let herself get caught up in something that wasn't real.

"Lea, I want you to know that I can't remember the last time I enjoyed myself this much. If I were to be stuck on a deserted island, I can't think of anyone else I'd want to be with."

Her heart definitely skipped a beat. "I feel the same way." Their gazes caught and held. Maybe she shouldn't have said that. Trying to lighten the mood, she glanced away. "After all, you know how to start a fire and—"

"Lea, will you marry me?"

"What?" Surely she hadn't heard him correctly.

"You heard me, will you marry me?"

Her mouth gaped. Where in the world had that come from? And then she wondered if he felt the need to do the right thing because she was pregnant. That had to be it, because there was no other reason for them to marry. It wasn't like they were in love or anything.

She appreciated how he'd phrased the offer as a question instead of making it a demand. Her parents never stopped to ask her opinion before dictating how things should be. They'd continued to treat her as a child until the day she packed up and caught a plane to Greece—her adventure to find out about the family she never knew existed.

And Charles, had he deemed her fit to be his wife, would have told her they were getting married instead of asking her. Thank goodness that never happened.

Lea shook her head. "It won't work."

"It can if we want it to."

"I won't marry someone I don't love."

The pain reflected in his eyes had her regretting her blunt answer. She just didn't want him holding out for something that wasn't going to happen.

Lea got up and moved to the water's edge. She knew she'd hurt him and that hadn't been her intention. But in the long run, this would be less painful for both of them.

CHAPTER THIRTEEN

LAST NIGHT HADN'T gone the way he'd planned it.

Not even close.

Xander had been frowning all day today—at least that was what Joseph had accused him of. Why did Lea's rejection sting so much? It wasn't like he was madly in love with her. He was just trying to make things easier for her—for both of them.

Because the baby needed them both. And for that reason, he wasn't giving up on changing Lea's mind about marrying him. He would give Lea and the child his name—it would get them a long way in life—plus a sizeable chunk of his fortune. And when the time came, the child would inherit his empire.

Xander, along with a work crew, finished putting a new roof on one of the bungalows. And since it was nearing lunchtime, he decided to ask Lea to share a meal with him. They had barely spoken since she'd turned down his marriage proposal. And now that the sting of her rejection had worn off, he had to take emotions out of the equation and focus on the end goal—creating a family for their baby.

As he walked from the bungalow to Lea's office,

he had to navigate through the throng of wedding guests. They were everywhere—there was even a line of people waiting to be seated at the Hideaway Café. That was a first. So much for his plan of a grabbing a decaf caramel latte for Lea as a peace offering.

Xander continued on to the main offices when he saw Lea step out into the sunshine, but she wasn't alone. She was with a middle-aged couple. The man carried a briefcase and the woman wore a dark skirt and jacket. They definitely weren't here for some romance in the sun and he highly doubted they were the bride and groom. So, who were they?

The smile slipped from his face. They were prospective buyers for the island. He was certain of it. Who knew so many people were interested in running a wedding island?

Suddenly it felt like all the progress he'd made with Lea was in jeopardy. The thought of at last having his own family—people he could trust— people that would always be there for him and him for them—was slipping through his fingers. And it was only then that he realized just how much he wanted this—wanted the family he hadn't known he could have.

He headed for Lea. He wasn't sure what he was going to say. He felt a little betrayed that as close as they were growing she still wouldn't consider accepting his help, but she would consider selling to strangers—people she didn't know she could trust with her beloved island.

"Please feel free to explore the island at your leisure," Lea said to the couple with her back to Xander.

"I just wouldn't take the boat tour, if I were you."

Lea immediately spun around and leveled a dark, warning stare at him. The look immediately brought him to his senses.

"And why would that be?" the man asked with a concerned look on his face.

Lea turned to the man. "It's nothing to worry about. Xander was just making a joke. It was something you had to be there to understand. But our boats are all well maintained and available should you like to see the island from the sea. Just let me know. If you'll excuse me for a moment, I need to have a quick word with Mr. Marinakos."

It was impossible to miss the anger written all over her face as she faced Xander. This time he had no one to blame but himself for taking quite a few steps back in their relationship. She led them a safe distance away from the couple she'd been talking to.

With her back turned to her guests, she said, "What do you think you're doing?"

"I was just trying to make a joke. Like you said."

Her gaze narrowed. "That was no joke. So what gives?"

She had called him out and maybe it was good to tell her the truth—all of it. After all, at this point, what could it hurt?

He swallowed. "I thought that you and I, we were growing closer."

She hesitated. "As friends."

They both knew their relationship had gone beyond friendship, but if it made her more comfortable to think of them as merely friends, he wasn't going to correct her.

He stared into her eyes. "I thought you were beginning to trust me."

"I… I am." He read confusion in her eyes. "But what does that have to do with you trying to run off prospective buyers? You know how important this is to me."

And he felt bad for letting himself act rashly. He raked his fingers through his hair. It wasn't something he ever allowed himself to do when he was conducting a business deal. In fact, he was more inclined to take his time and let the other man sweat it out. But with Lea and the baby on the line, he was the one sweating out how this was all going to work out.

"I thought by now you'd realize you could trust me—that you would consider letting me give…" He paused. This wasn't coming out right. If he didn't handle this correctly, she would dig her heels in even deeper. He sighed and lowered his head. "Never mind. I'm sorry I interrupted your meeting."

He turned to walk away when she reached out, touching his arm. "Xander, wait."

He glanced back to her, not sure what he expected her to say. He remained quiet, letting her have her say.

Her gaze searched his. "What were you hoping would happen?" She didn't give him a chance to answer as she barreled forward. "Were you hoping that if you sweet-talked me on a deserted beach I would suddenly decide to sell to you?"

"No." His voice was sterner than he'd intended it to be. He made an effort to soften his voice. "I'd hoped you'd let me loan you the money to fix up the island."

"With strings—"

"No. No strings attached." It wasn't how he normally did business, but he'd make an exception in this case. "It would be because we're friends."

She stepped closer to him, never breaking eye contact. "You're being serious, aren't you?"

He let out a breath he hadn't even realized that he'd been holding. "Yes, I am."

"After all of this time, you still don't get it."

His brows drew together. "Get what?"

"That what this baby needs from you isn't money. It needs you to let down your guard and love it. He or she needs you to be an active part of its life."

Xander took a step back. She was asking him to be a loving, devoted parent. And as much as he wanted that, too, he was afraid he'd follow the parenting examples from his past. "I'm not good with emotions."

"Is that what your sister would say? I see the way your eyes light up when you talk about her. You'd do anything for her, wouldn't you?"

"Of course, but that's different—"

"You love her, right?"

"Yes. But—"

"But you're willing to give your child less?"

His back teeth ground together. Why was she twisting his words around on him? He was doing what was best for the child—protecting it from him.

Lea pleaded with her eyes. "You don't have to follow your father's example. Be the understanding, encouraging parent you always wanted him to be." She glanced over her shoulder at her waiting guests. "I have to go."

Xander had come here hoping to get through to her, but as she walked away, it was the other way around. Was she right? Could he be the father that he'd always longed for?

* * *

Should she trust him?

Lea's heart said yes. But her mind said no.

After all, he'd attempted to sabotage the sale with the couple today. She stood off to the side of the dock, watching the continuous arrival of guests for the royal wedding. She spotted the couple as they boarded the ferry and waved to them. As interested as they had been in the island and the wedding business, in the end they'd said that the island was more of a time commitment than they were willing to invest at this point in their lives. And so they'd passed on the chance to own Infinity Island.

They had seemed like the perfect buyers. The husband was all about numbers and spreadsheets and processes while his wife was more focused on the people and the romance and the weddings. Lea couldn't have asked for a better match for the island. And yet, it hadn't worked out. And it wasn't until now that she realized deep down she didn't want it to work out.

She loved Infinity Island. It was a part of her. And the harder she tried to sell it, the more she realized how much she wanted to keep it.

But she also had the baby to think of. Her hand covered her baby bump. She had to do what was right for her baby, no matter what she had to sacrifice. Even her pride.

And returning to Seattle, the land where she'd been born and raised, the place where she had friends and family, and knew exactly how things worked, might be best. Because as much as she loved this island, it was part of a country that she still had so much to learn about—including the language. There were so many obstacles to overcome if she were to stay here. And staying on in Athens would just be a reminder of how she'd come here and failed to live up to her extended family's expectations.

So if she were to go home, she should try to reach out to her parents. They had a right to know they were going to be grandparents. Xander's words of regret over his parents came to her. She didn't want to live with regrets like him. And if she couldn't forgive her parents, how was she going to be a good mother?

Lea picked up the phone and dialed the familiar number of her parents' home. The phone rang and rang. When the answering machine picked up, she hung up. She thought of calling her mother's cell phone but hesitated. Again, she recalled Xander encouraging her not to give up. She dialed the number. It went to voice mail. She disconnected.

She was not going to have this conversation via a message. To be honest, she wasn't sure if her mother was truly busy or if she was avoiding her call. Her mother would see the missed phone call and could call back if she wanted. Lea had made the first move, now her mother could make a move...or not.

Lea shut down her computer in order to head home a little early to prepare for the royal wedding. For the past year, she'd been spending all of her time working from first thing in the morning until late at night when she fell into bed utterly exhausted, but then again, until now she hadn't had anyone waiting at home for her. The thought of Xander had her moving faster.

"Hey, where are you headed so quickly?"

Lea stopped on the walk outside the office and turned to Popi. "I was just going home to get ready."

"The wedding is going to be the highlight of the year. But aren't you leaving a little early to get dressed?" Popi made a big show of checking the time on her phone.

"I, um, finished everything early."

"Uh-huh." Popi nodded and sent her a knowing smile. "I bet I know what has you rushing home. Or should I say who?"

"It's not like that." The response was quick—too quick. They both knew she was lying.

"You keep telling yourself that. It's kinda like telling myself that I'm not pregnant." Popi placed a hand on her expanding midsection. "The bigger I get the more I wonder about the delivery and whether this was my wisest decision."

"It's a little late for second thoughts, don't you think?"

Popi gave a nervous laugh. "You would be right. But doesn't it scare you to think of delivering a baby?"

"I'll be honest. I try not to think about it." It probably wasn't the best approach, but she was not looking forward to the pain. "Why exactly are we talking about this anyway?"

"I think we were originally talking about Xander and your eagerness to see him. I'm glad to see that things are going better for you two." Popi got a serious look on her face. "This is a good thing, isn't it?"

Lea smiled and nodded. "It's good. This baby needs two parents that get along."

"If it changes, I'm here to talk, eat gelato and watch movies."

"Thanks. You're the best."

As they parted company, Lea realized Popi was as close to her as what she imagined a sister would be. She was going to miss her so much when she left here.

She didn't have long to think about it before Xander joined her.

He made point of checking the time. "What are you up to? It's not quitting time."

"Would you believe me if I said I was looking for you?"

"It's a little late to ask me to lunch. And it's too early for dinner."

"I had something else in mind." Her stomach felt like a swarm of butterflies had been set loose in it.

He gave her a puzzled look. "You're in a really good mood."

"I am." She didn't know why she was. It wasn't exactly a good day. The sale hadn't gone through. She hadn't gotten hold of her mother. And her email inbox was overflowing with unread messages. Not to mention all the bills that were beginning to stack up. But she refused to think of all that now.

His expression was neutral but his gaze never left her. "So your business deal, it went well?"

"Actually, it fell through."

"If I had anything to do with it—"

She shook her head. "You didn't. The island was too much of a time commitment for them."

"And still you're in a good mood, why?"

She shrugged. She refused to delve too deeply into the reason for her happiness. "It's a beautiful day. It's the end of the week. And there's about to be a royal wedding. Isn't that a good enough reason?"

He shrugged. "Works for me." They walked for

a few minutes in silence. "What do you say about having dinner together? But this evening there will be no mention of marriage. Just two friends having a good time together."

"Can I ask you something?"

"Are you trying to change the subject?"

"No. I just want to know something before I give you my answer."

"Should I be worried?"

She shrugged. "Depends on how you look at it."

"What's your question?"

"Why are you still here? Why are you fixing up the island? Why do you want to have dinner with me?"

He stopped walking and turned to her. "Why do you think?"

"I think it's all about the baby." Inside she was begging him to prove her wrong.

"Is that what you want?"

No. No. No. He wasn't supposed to turn her question around on her. "That's not an answer."

He sighed and pressed his hands to his waist. "Is it so hard to believe that I want to spend time with you, not because I want to buy the island and not because you're having my baby, but because I like you? I like your company."

She couldn't hold back the smile that lifted her lips. "You do?"

"I do. I… I like you a lot and I would like to see

where this thing between us is leading. So how about that dinner?"

"I'd love to, but I'm afraid there's a wedding and reception shortly. In fact, I was just heading home to change and head over to the festivities."

"Do you attend each and every wedding?"

"I must admit that I don't. My schedule doesn't always allow me. But I make a point to attend as many as I can. And this royal wedding is an all-hands-on-deck affair. Besides, there's something so rewarding about seeing two hearts joined together for infinity." She smiled. "It's something very special and lets me know that what I do here plays some small part in two people becoming one."

"That does sound very fulfilling. It isn't something I've ever experienced with my work. Deals are usually made in boardrooms and it's a matter of business. At most, there's a handshake and a smile, but there's no joy. From the sound of it, I've been missing out on some things."

What was he trying to tell her? Was he saying he wanted to change his life? Impossible. He was one of the world's most successful people. When they made those lists of the richest people, he was at the top of it, year after year. And she knew he enjoyed his work. So what was he trying to say?

"Any chance I can convince you to skip it?"

She sent him a look that said "Are you serious?". "No."

"I didn't think so." There was a noticeable pause before he asked, "How about I tag along with you?"

"You want to crash a wedding?" She didn't think it could be possible but things were getting even stranger.

He smiled. "I confess—it's something I've never done."

"And you plan to get all dressed up?"

"My suit from when I first arrived was sent to the dry cleaners and is now hanging in my closet, all set to go."

She was running out of ideas to reject this as a bad idea. And it would be fun to show Xander why she cared so much about the island. The happiness, the joy and the hope found at these celebrations was inspiring. It kept her wanting to do better and help more people have a smooth trip down the aisle.

"Let's do it." She smiled before setting off side by side with him on their wedding date.

CHAPTER FOURTEEN

WHAT IN THE world had come over him?

Xander couldn't believe he was willingly attending a wedding and reception—and it wasn't even for anyone he knew. These days he made a point of not attending weddings. In his experience, women had a way of turning the occasion into much more than a nice evening out. He'd always told himself that romantic commitments weren't for him.

But to have a date with Lea, to hold her in his arms—he would agree to most anything just to spend time with her, even walking over hot coals. Thankfully that was not a part of the evening's festivities. And it wasn't like Lea expected anything from him. She'd made that perfectly clear the other night.

And boy, was she a knockout tonight with that little black dress on. A silver satin sash around her waist accentuated her curves, including her baby bump. The black lace bodice teased him with glimpses of her cleavage. He definitely had the most beautiful woman at the wedding on his arm—too bad for the prince.

Not having to worry about meeting any romantic expectations, Xander found himself relaxing and enjoying Lea's company. And when she'd finally coerced him onto the dance floor, he was envisioning a slow dance where he could pull her into his arms nice and close.

Instead, after they were already on the dance floor, an upbeat song started to play. It was something he'd never heard before, but seeing as the bride was American, it didn't surprise him. Lea's face beamed with happiness. She was most definitely in her element here. And then people formed a big circle. The next thing he knew, they were all flapping their arms and wiggling their backsides.

He stood perfectly still, having no clue what was going on. Lea had nudged him and told him it was called the Chicken Dance. *Whatever that is.* Lea encouraged him to join in. He did so reluctantly.

He might be on a vacation of sorts, but he was still a businessman. He inwardly cringed, thinking of a video of this going viral. He had to watch out for his reputation and this…this dance was not the least bit sensical. But it did cause Lea to smile and laugh. That was worth his bit of discomfort.

But his efforts to make Lea happy were soon rewarded with a slow song. At last, he'd wrapped his arms around her. The soft hint of floral perfume teased his senses. As they moved around the floor, it was as if no one else existed. All he had eyes for was her. And then somewhere along the way, their gazes had locked. His heart pounded against his ribs.

There was something special about Lea. It went deeper than her carrying his baby. He'd dated many women in his life—beautiful, famous, rich women. None of them had made him reconsider the set of rules by which he lived his life. None made him want to open up and share not only his accomplishments but also his hopes, failures and deepest regrets.

But did Lea feel the same way toward him?

The memory of his rejected marriage proposal lingered in the back of his mouth with a sour taste. Maybe he'd had too much wine that evening. That had to be why he was rehashing the failed proposal. Otherwise he wouldn't even be considering further pursuit of this woman, who'd snuck past his elaborate walls, who filled his thoughts both day and night.

It was then that he had to confront the truth—he wanted more from Lea than an amicable friendship—more than a convenient marriage. He was still struggling for the words to describe his vision for their future, but in this moment, none were needed. He'd swooped in for a kiss. It was short and sweet. He didn't want to push his luck as the evening was going perfectly.

But now, as they walked home, he couldn't help recalling the softness of her lips against his. Even though the kiss had been brief, it had sparked a fire within him that continued to smolder. He ached for more of her. So much more.

Xander continued to hold Lea's hand. "Thank you for this evening. The wedding wasn't bad after all."

"Wasn't bad? As I seem to recall, you had a rather good time. You were even laughing during the Chicken Dance."

"Such a ridiculous name for something that in no way resembles a dance."

"It's a lot of fun and helps loosen up the crowd. Seemed to work just fine to get you to relax and enjoy the rest of the evening."

"I don't know if flapping my arms relaxed me, but I did enjoy the rest of the evening. We'll have to crash another wedding sometime."

He didn't say it but it wasn't the dance that had him enjoying this evening, it was her. Lea was the most amazing woman in the world. Beneath the moonlight, he stumbled upon another moment of clarity. If he let Lea get away, there would never be anyone nearly as special—as perfect—for him.

Lea's sigh drew his attention.

"What's on your mind?" He wanted to know anything and everything about her.

"I was just thinking that there won't be another time. At least not here on the island." She sounded saddened by the thought. "Not if I sell it."

It saddened him, too. But he didn't want to rehash the subject of the island. He knew it would lead to nothing but trouble for them. And he wasn't about to ruin this evening.

He needed to change the subject. "Have you talked with your parents?"

They continued to stroll along at a leisurely pace. "Actually, I took your advice and tried."

"Tried?"

She nodded. "No one answered. And no one has called back, so I don't know what to make of it."

"Did you leave a message?"

"Um, no." She avoided his searching gaze.

"How are they supposed to know to call, if you didn't leave a message?"

"They'll see a missed call and my number."

He didn't say a word. Instead he shook his head.

"Why are you shaking your head? At least I tried. It's more than they've done."

She did have a point. "That's true. Maybe they're traveling. Or out of cell reception."

"My parents don't travel. They love their little corner of the world."

"When did you call?"

"This afternoon, before I left the office."

That would explain why she'd repeatedly checked her phone during the evening. He had started to think that he had been boring her.

Xander squeezed her hand. "Give it time. They'll call."

"Maybe." But she didn't sound convinced.

He knew what it was like to have your family let you down—except his sister. Stasia had always been there for him, even when he didn't want her to be. These days she seemed to think he needed to settle down and start a family of his own. He wondered what she'd think of him making a family with Lea.

"You have to understand," Lea said, drawing his full attention, "my relationship with them is quite strained. My mother thinks she always knows best. She's been making decisions for me my whole life. Like my college, I didn't even know about all the schools that had accepted me until it was too late. But the final straw was when she kept my extended family from me. Do you even know what that felt like?"

"I have some idea." His adoptive parents had never kept it a secret that he was adopted. When he was young, his mother would say he was the child they chose—the child of their hearts. That reassurance had faded away after his little sister came along.

Lea's eyes widened. "Of course you do. I'm sorry. I shouldn't make a big deal of this."

"Don't diminish your feelings just because of me. You have a right to those feelings."

"I just don't know how my parents could look me in the face after what they'd done. And instead of apologizing, they said they'd done the right thing and that they would do it again. That wasn't their decision to make. They acted like my relatives were a bunch of criminals. And nothing could be further from the truth."

"Maybe your parents were afraid you would leave them."

"That's still no excuse. It didn't have to be an either-or decision, but in the end they made it one. And now...now I don't know if my baby, um, our baby will know its grandparents."

"But I thought you were moving home." Was there a chance she'd changed her mind? Was she considering making her life here in Greece—close to him?

Lea stopped just outside the door to their bungalow and turned to him. "I haven't decided. Just because I return to the States doesn't mean I'll live near my parents. I could live in downtown Seattle, where I went to college. I still have friends from school there."

He reached out and gently traced his finger down the side of her beautiful face. "Or you could stay here where you have friends that care about you. And you'll have me."

She lifted her chin until their gazes met. "Do you care about me?"

For a second, his heart stilled. She was calling him out—making him confess feelings that he hadn't even admitted to himself. But if he wanted her to stay—to make a family with him—then he was going to have to take the biggest risk of his life.

He swallowed hard. "Yes. I care about you. And I want you to stay."

She didn't turn away. Her eyes widened with surprise. Had he kept his evolving feelings so far under wraps? For him, it felt like his heart had been hanging on his sleeve. It was a new feeling—a vulnerability that he'd never allowed himself to feel until now.

She continued to stare into his eyes as though searching for the truth of his words. He leaned down and pressed a kiss to her lips. He wasn't sure how she would react.

At first, she stood unmoving, as though she were in shock by his admission. Maybe he was acting too swiftly. Perhaps he should slow this down and let her absorb what he'd said to her.

He started to pull back, but her hands moved with lightning speed. Her fingers clutched the lapels of his jacket, pulling him back to her. This time she took the lead. As her mouth opened to him, his tongue delved inside, tasting the sweetness of the champagne from the wedding reception.

But it was her kiss that was intoxicating. His hold on her waist tightened. Her curves fit so perfectly against his. As their kiss deepened, he realized he would never get enough of this—enough of Lea.

Hand in hand they stepped inside the bungalow. Not bothering with the lights, they headed straight for Lea's bedroom.

With the moonlight filtering in through the window and illuminating them, Xander stared at Lea. She was so beautiful. He was the luckiest man in the world.

His heart raced and his need to pull her close mounted. But there was something he needed to say first. "Lea, is tonight what you want? What you really want?"

She nodded. Her gaze never strayed from his. "You are everything I've ever wanted."

His head dipped, and he claimed her lips. No one had ever said those words to him or made him feel the way she did. He was falling hard for her.

Correction: he'd already fallen head over heels.

CHAPTER FIFTEEN

"I CAN'T LEAVE NOW."

Xander gripped the phone tightly as his sister insisted he drop everything and fly to Italy. Normally he would do anything for Stasia, but after spending the night with Lea in his arms, he felt torn between his brotherly responsibility and cementing this blossoming relationship with Lea.

"I don't understand this," his sister said. "What could possibly be more important than business? I swear it's the only reason you get out of bed in the morning."

Xander raked his fingers through his hair. He had yet to tell his sister about Lea and the baby. He still felt protective of the relationship and didn't want to expose it to other peoples' criticisms.

"Maybe it's time I take some time for myself," he said, hoping she'd drop the subject.

"Hmph…" His sister didn't sound convinced. "So you're trying to tell me that you're on vacation?"

"Yes." He jumped at the answer, perhaps a little too quickly. "I've decided I need to slow down a bit."

"Uh-huh. And where would you be vacationing?"

"In the Mediterranean. On an island."

"Could you be any more obscure? I mean, what if there's an emergency and I need you."

Since their parents had passed on, there was just the two of them. "You can call my cell phone."

"Xander."

In his mind, he could imagine his sister with her hip thrown to the side with a hand resting on it while she glared at him for being difficult. She'd mastered that posture when they were kids and it still worked on him.

"Fine. I'm on Infinity Island."

His sister gasped. "You're on a wedding island? You're getting married and you didn't tell me?"

"No. No. Calm down." He couldn't believe his sister had heard of the island. Apparently it was renowned, just like Lea said.

"Well, what else would you be doing there? People only go there to get married or attend a wedding. And I know you hate going to weddings because you feel awkward attending solo and you don't want to ask any of your lady friends to be your date because they might get the wrong idea and start thinking you're open to making a commitment. So what gives?"

Xander really did want someone to bounce ideas off. And his sister might be able to lend some advice where Lea was concerned. And the truth was Stasia was going to learn of the pregnancy eventually. He'd rather it came from him.

"Initially, I came to Infinity Island to buy it."

"I take it that's not why you're there now."

He shook his head before realizing that she couldn't see him. "No. It's something more personal. Lea is pregnant."

"Who is Lea?"

He went on to explain how he'd gotten to know Lea and the fun time they'd had together.

"Pregnant? Wow," Stasia said. "I didn't see that coming. I didn't even know you wanted a family."

"I didn't know I did either, not until there was a baby. And now all I can think about is the three of us becoming a family."

"Xander, slow down. Are you even sure the baby is yours?"

"Yes." He said it without hesitation.

"How much do you know about this woman? Have you done a background check?"

"Stasia, I'm not doing that. What I need to know, I'll learn from her."

"Xander, think about this. You barely know this woman. How do you know she's not running a scam—"

"Because I know her. Stasia, I told you this because I wanted to share this information with my sister. But if you can't be happy for me, stay out of it."

Strained silence greeted him. He may love his sister, but she had to respect his relationship with Lea.

"Xander, I didn't mean to upset you. It's just that you're my brother and I love you. I don't want you to be hurt. That's all."

Xander smiled. "I know."

"Promise me you won't go rushing into anything."

"Don't worry. I've got this." He ended the conversation by promising to call soon.

Now that he was certain he could make this thing with Lea work, he knew words wouldn't be enough to prove his commitment to her. He had to back up his words with action—something that would show Lea just how serious he was about making them into a family of three.

CHAPTER SIXTEEN

AN INTERESTED BUYER...

A lot of mixed emotions came over Lea. Whereas, at one point, she'd thought that selling the island was her only option, now she wondered if she'd been too quick. And did she really want to move back to Seattle after making a life for herself here with so many people around that cared about her?

Her thoughts circled back around to her parents and how they hadn't returned her call. Sure, she hadn't left a message, but the missed call would have shown up on the cell phone. After all, she'd reached out first. That had to count for something.

But their lingering silence was unexpected. Lea didn't realize how deeply their unhappiness with her went. Right then and there she promised herself that she'd never do something like that with her child. A love fiercer than she'd ever known came over her. She wouldn't let anyone or anything come between her and her child.

"Hey. Hello." Popi waved at Lea to get her attention. "What has you so deep in thought?"

Lea gave herself a mental shake. "Sorry. What did you say?"

"I stopped by to ask if you wanted to go over the plans for the upcoming wedding."

These weddings weren't just your normal weddings. They were dreams brought to life. And in some cases, they took a lot of construction.

"Remind me of the details?"

Popi gave her a strange look. "It isn't like you to forget details."

Lea sighed and leaned back in her chair. "I've had a lot on my mind lately."

"You mean that tall, sexy guy sharing your bungalow has you distracted."

Lea frowned at her friend. "I meant the business."

Though Popi was partially right. When Lea wasn't thinking about what to do with the island, her mind was on Xander and how every time he kissed her, it felt like the first time. She lost touch with reality and her feet no longer touched the earth.

Popi nodded in understanding. "Have you eaten lunch yet?"

Lea shook her head. Ever since she'd heard there was another buyer interested in the island, she'd been utterly distracted. As much as she loved the island, if she found a buyer that loved it as much as she did and was capable of fixing it up the way it should be, Lea knew the right thing would be to turn the island over. It would be what was best for everyone. Wouldn't it?

Popi signaled for her to join her. "Come on. Our babies would probably appreciate the nourishment."

Lea arched a brow at Popi. She was worried her friend was going to get too attached to her niece or nephew and have a hard time handing it over to its parents. Popi assured her that wouldn't happen but it didn't keep Lea from worrying. Lea couldn't imagine ever parting with the little one inside her.

"Stop worrying," Popi said. "I'm not getting attached."

"Uh-huh." Lea didn't believe her and she doubted that Popi believed her own words.

"I'm serious. I know this is my niece or nephew. And...and I'm glad I won't be the one stumbling around in the middle of the night with a crying baby."

As they made their way to the nearby café, Popi changed the subject. "So, what are your plans?"

Lea's eyes lit up with interest. "Plans for what?"

"Mr. Hot & Sexy. Are you going to ride off into the sunset with him?"

"No. Of course not." Although he had asked her to marry him. But he hadn't really meant it. It had sounded more like a business proposition than anything else. Not wanting to talk about Xander and all of her mixed-up emotions where he was concerned, she said, "But I do have news."

"Spill it."

"I have an interested buyer for the island. And I think this woman has real potential to be the right fit. We talked on the phone this morning for quite some time. She had so many questions. She was interested in all aspects of the island."

Popi paused outside the café. A worried look came over her face. "After walking away from your life—from your family—to claim your heritage, are you ready to give it up so quickly?"

"I have to do what is best."

"Best for whom?"

Lea's gaze met her friend's. "Don't worry. I'll make sure whoever buys the island keeps the staff. You don't have to worry. I'll make it part of the sales agreement."

"That's not what I'm worried about, but thank you."

The meeting with the potential buyer was in the morning. After Xander had been so reckless in front of her other potential buyers, she wasn't about to tell him about this one. But she needed to make sure he was distracted.

"Would you mind if Xander helped you with some of the reception details?" Lea asked.

Popi gave her a puzzled look. "We have enough staff to handle the job."

"I know. I just need him kept busy for the morning. That prospective buyer is flying in."

"Oh. Okay. No problem."

"Thank you so much."

"Any time. I'm always here for you."

That was the truth, and another reason Lea so desperately wanted to stay on the island. But what was she willing to do to make that happen?

Something was up with Lea.

He was certain of it.

The following day, Xander was bothered by something Lea had said the previous evening. She'd tried to get him to go with Popi to the other side of the island to set up for a jungle-themed wedding reception. Normally he'd have volunteered, but after working on the island, he'd learned a lot and he knew the staging crew wasn't shorthanded. In fact, he'd more than likely get in their way rather than be of any help. So what had been Lea's purpose for the request?

She'd brought it up again that morning, but he'd told her he already had plans. And that was no lie. He was working on his surprise for her. Or was that it? Had she figured out what he was up to?

He mulled it over for much of the morning and then decided she didn't know because she would have said something. Lea was up to something—something that she didn't want him to know about. And for the life of him, he couldn't get the thought out of his mind.

With the nursery well underway, he decided to

meet up with Lea just to make sure everything was all right between them. He headed toward her office where she spent a lot of her day. It seemed strange to him that living on this sunny, beautiful island she would be stuck inside much of the time. If his office was here, he'd make sure he was mobile. He'd take his laptop and spend as much time working outside as possible.

He really could imagine himself working here. This place and the people that lived and worked on the island felt more like a small, close-knit community than business associates.

As he walked toward the office, he considered inviting Lea to lunch. But it should be something more than lunch at one of the cafés. Perhaps they could get their lunch to go and have it down along the beach. The more he thought about it, the more the details came into focus.

He was almost to the office when he saw Lea exit the building, but she wasn't alone. There was a woman with her. They were talking and laughing. When the woman turned so that he could see her face, he came to a complete standstill.

Stasia?

What was she doing here?

He immediately knew the answer. His little sister was here to check out the woman who was going to have his baby. Stasia had to make sure Lea was good enough.

He shook his head in disbelief. His sister had crossed the line. He could just imagine her interrogating Lea. He was going to put a stop to it—

"Xander, there you are."

He didn't want to stop. He didn't want to talk to anyone but his sister. But he recognized the voice. It was Popi.

He paused and turned back. "Can we talk later? I was just about to—"

"It's really important. There's an emergency."

He searched her face to see if she was being serious. And by all accounts, Popi did look worried. "What's wrong?"

"There was an accident this morning. It's Joseph. I think he broke his leg."

"Is that why I heard the helicopter?"

"Not exactly. They delivered a visitor and were on standby when the accident occurred."

He didn't have to ask to know that his sister was the one to fly onto the island. Stasia wasn't wasting any time vetting the new woman in his life. But in the end, he supposed it wasn't all bad as the helicopter was already on the island, saving lots of time getting Joseph to the hospital.

"What can I do to help?"

"There's still lots of work to be done and I'm looking for any able bodies to help. We're running out of time."

He glanced over his shoulder to where he'd last

seen Lea and his sister. They had moved out of sight. Confronting Stasia would have to wait.

And so would the nursery that he had just about finished. He hadn't even been sure that he'd be able to pull it off with Lea sleeping at the other end of the hallway. But by some miracle, he'd been able to get most of the sawing and hammering done while she was at the office.

And if by chance that wasn't enough to prove to her that he was serious about them—about their family—he was in the process of having plans drawn up to relocate his offices to the island. He never thought that he'd be happy living outside of the city—with his thumb on the heartbeat of commerce—but Lea had changed all of that.

Now he couldn't imagine living away from Lea and their child. And there was something about Infinity Island—something that felt like home.

CHAPTER SEVENTEEN

THERE WAS A buyer for the island.

And now she had to truly decide where her future lay.

Lea knew selling the island would be hard, but she hadn't realized it would be this hard. Even though the woman she'd met with the previous day was really nice, very interested in the island and had promised to keep it running in the same manner as Lea's ancestors had done, Lea was still hesitant to sell.

Selling Infinity Island would be giving up on her heritage—giving up on her friends that were now her family, giving up on finding out if this thing with Xander was real. It sure felt real to her, but she didn't know if Xander felt the same way.

Xander was offering her a chance to have everything she'd ever wanted. And he'd done everything to show her how invested he was in this relationship. Now it was time she met him halfway. It was time she took a chance with the island and most of all, with her heart.

As soon as she arrived at the office, she called the number the woman had left her. It went to voice mail. Lea didn't really want to leave this information in a voice mail.

She attempted to work, but her mind just wasn't into it. She was so excited about what the future held. Teaming up with Xander would be interesting. She believed that there was nothing they couldn't do together.

Just before ten o'clock in the morning, Lea gave up the pretense of working. She planned to swing by the bungalow and switch into more sensible shoes before she went to track down Xander at whatever project he'd gotten involved with this time. With Joseph laid up for a couple of months, there was more work than ever to be done.

Lea stepped through the doorway of the bungalow, surprised to find Xander at home. He was video-chatting with his back to her. She slipped off her shoes at the door and walked softly across the floor, not wanting to disturb him. But she had to pass by the table in order to get to her room.

As she neared him, she heard a woman's voice. It was a familiar voice. Wait, she knew that voice. She couldn't quite place it.

It was best to keep walking, ignoring the woman's voice. But an uneasy feeling chewed away at her insides. Was there another woman in Xander's life?

And then the woman laughed. It was a warm, jingly kind of laugh. Xander replied softly to her, making it impossible for Lea to make out the words. The feeling in her gut turned to red hot jealousy. It was unmistakable. But she refused to let Xander know how she felt. She kept walking, but she couldn't resist a quick glance at his monitor.

Gasp!

Lea stopped. That was the same woman that had been interested in purchasing the island. But how could that be? Was Xander plotting against her?

Xander turned around. Surprise was written all over his handsome face. "Lea. Wait." He turned back to the computer. "I'll call you when I'm on the plane." And with that he closed the laptop.

By then Lea had recovered enough from the shock to get her feet to move. She thought about leaving, but then realized this was her home. She wasn't going anywhere. Xander was the one who was leaving. Hadn't she heard him say something about a plane?

She headed to the kitchen. She could hear his footsteps behind her. She steeled herself, refusing to let him see just how deeply his betrayal had hurt her.

"Lea, it's not what you think. That was my sister—"

"Stop. I don't want to hear whatever you have to say." She turned on him. Her shock morphed into anger. "What I think is that you and your sister made a fool of me. And now it's time you leave the island."

"No one made a fool of you. And no one set out to hurt you." He stepped closer to her.

She held her arm straight out, blocking his progress. "Just stay away. Don't try and charm your way out of this."

"Lea, don't do this. We can work everything out. I... I just need to take care of something first."

What could possibly be more important than this? And then she realized the foolishness of her question. It had to be business. It always came back to his business, whether it was trying to sweet-talk her out of the land or sending his sister in to do his dirty work.

"Just go." She turned her back to him.

"Lea, please believe me. I would never do anything to hurt you, but if I don't go, my company will be put in jeopardy from a large lawsuit. Please say you'll wait here for me. And then we can talk."

She turned back to him. "I'll be here. I'll always be here. But you won't be welcome."

She didn't need to hear anything else he had to say. He'd been keeping things from her, just like her parents had kept information about her family and her heritage from her. And they all had their excuses, but none of them were reason enough to keep Lea in the dark.

"I'll be back. I promise."

His words fell on deaf ears because she refused to believe anything he had to say from here on out.

If she needed any further proof that he wouldn't change—that he would always put business ahead of his family—this was it.

Frustration, pain and anger churned within her. After Xander left, she needed to do something, anything. But she couldn't concentrate enough to go back to the office. Instead she started to clean out her kitchen cabinets. She'd been meaning to do it for a long time now but had put it off for one reason or another.

She'd inherited all of this stuff. Some of the dishes were in amazing condition. Others had most definitely seen better days. She kept working, pulling everything out and sorting out the keepers and those that could go.

When her phone rang, she considered ignoring it. If it was Xander, she had absolutely no interest in talking to him. And if it was Popi, she didn't want to get into this with her, not yet. But she realized that it could be island business and that was something she couldn't ignore. And she refused to think how her priorities were similar to Xander's.

She glanced at the caller ID and her heart stopped. It was her mother. After an entire year, her mother was calling her. Was she returning her call? *But it has been so long.* Or had something happened? Was her father ill? *Please say it isn't so.*

Lea knew that all she would have were unanswered questions unless she accepted the call. Not giving herself time to think of all the reasons that this was a bad idea, she pressed the answer button on her phone.

"Hello."

"Lea? Is that you?"

"Yes, Mom. It's me." Her insides shivered with nerves. "Is something wrong with Dad?"

"Um…no, he's fine. I'm returning your call. I'm so sorry we missed it. My battery died just after we left on an Alaskan cruise so we had to rely on your father's phone."

"Dad has a cell phone? I thought he was opposed to them as they are a nuisance."

Her mother sighed. "A lot has changed since you left."

"A lot has changed here, too." It wasn't until she heard her mother's voice that she realized how much she missed speaking to her.

And as much as she'd worried about how things would go when she finally spoke to her mother again, they quickly fell into a comfortable conversation. It was almost like nothing had happened. And Lea opened up about the baby, Xander and the island being in trouble.

"You have a lot on your shoulders," her mother said. "I'm sorry about adding to your worries. Neither your father nor I meant to hurt you. We honestly thought we were saving you from more pain by being rejected by my family. I know what it feels like to be turned away and told I was dead to them for marrying a man they didn't approve of."

That was more information than Lea had gotten before, but that might have been because she'd been so upset with her parents that she hadn't let them say much. Lea told her mother that she regretted leaving Seattle in such a huff and not calling. Her mother apologized, too.

"But what will you do about Xander?" her mother asked. "Will you hear him out?"

"I... I don't know. I trusted him and he hurt me. Can you imagine him asking his sister to come here pretending to be a prospective buyer?"

Her mother was quiet for a moment. "I know you don't want to hear this, especially after what happened between us, but is there a chance he had good intentions?"

"Mom..."

"Wait. Listen to me and then you can ignore everything I say." Her mother paused as though waiting to see if she had Lea's attention. "Perhaps you were expecting him to let you down because other people, especially me, have let you down in the past. Could that be part of it?"

Lea heard her mother, and as much as she wanted to disagree with her, she remained quiet. She had a lot of thinking to do because there was a baby relying on her to make the right decision—for both of them.

CHAPTER EIGHTEEN

"I'LL MEET YOU in Rome with the car and all of the documents."

Xander stood at the airport listening to Roberto, his second in charge, go over everything that needed to happen to head off the possibility of his sister losing her entire life's savings and putting his company in jeopardy—the company that he'd worked all his life to make the biggest and the best.

But as Roberto continued to speak, Xander's mind was not on business. It was on the devastated look he'd seen on Lea's face when he left. And then the truth of the matter struck him with the strength of a lightning strike, nearly knocking him off his feet and into a nearby chair. He'd done everything wrong.

His heart just wasn't in this business deal or heading off a business bully. In the past, there was nothing he'd have liked better than proving to a business opponent that they were wrong. But now, things had changed.

His heart was back on Infinity Island with Lea and their baby.

"Xander, did you hear me?"

He hadn't heard a word the man had said in

the last couple of minutes. "Listen Roberto, we're going to change things."

"Change things? Now? We don't have time."

"We always have time to do the right thing."

Roberto paused as though confused. "We are doing the right thing. We're right and they are wrong. We just have to prove it and quickly."

Until this point, Xander had always taken a hands-on approach with his business. Until now, he hadn't imagined ever letting someone else be in charge of his company—not even long enough to take a vacation. Until Lea, his life had been his work. And now all of that had changed.

As Roberto talked in his ear, Xander realized that he had a very competent and eager number two. Due to Xander's need to be in control of everything, big and small, Roberto hadn't gotten a chance to spread his wings. Until now…

"Roberto."

The man stuttered to a halt.

"I appreciate all the work you've done. Over the years and most especially on this project. You appear to know all of the details. And you understand what I hope to accomplish."

"Uh… Thank you, sir."

Xander realized he'd really held onto the reins of the office too tightly. He noticed how Lea ran the island with a much more relaxed attitude. Perhaps it was time he did the same, especially if his plans worked out.

"Call me Xander."

"Yes, sir. Erm, Xander."

Xander smiled. He could tell this transformation was going to take time for everyone to adjust to. And then Xander went on to tell Roberto that he was the one going to Italy to represent the company.

"Are you sure?" Roberto asked.

"If you'd asked me that question a year ago, even a month ago, I would have said no. But a lot has changed to open my eyes. You're ready for this—you're more than ready. You probably know the facts and figures of this project better than I do at this point."

"Where will you be?"

"I'm heading back to Infinity Island. I left some unfinished business there."

He just hoped Lea would hear him out. He should have made more of an effort to tell her about his sister. He'd never meant for her to learn the truth the way she did.

And he had no idea what he was going to do if they couldn't work their way past this.

CHAPTER NINETEEN

ONE MINUTE SHE was certain they had no future.

The next moment, she missed him with all her heart.

Lea expelled a huff as she paced back and forth in the bungalow. With each pass, the walls felt as though they were closing in on her. She needed to keep herself occupied.

And she didn't feel like going to the office. However, she did feel like some good old-fashioned hard work—like cleaning. It'd been quite a while since she gave the place a thorough spring cleaning. And with the kitchen done, she might as well keep going.

Lea started toward her bedroom to strip her bed and throw the linen in the wash, when she came to a pause outside Xander's room. Not that it was actually his room. In fact, it was as good a time as any to clean away any lingering memories of him.

She opened the door and stepped inside. Her gaze took in the pastel green and purple walls. *What in the world?*

There was a new light fixture. New windows and curtains. There were even new closet doors that worked, unlike the old ones. And inside the closet, she found shelves above the clothes rod. Plenty of room for the baby's things.

Lea's vision blurred and she quickly blinked away the tears. She turned and took in all of the baby furniture. It was the wooden cradle that called to her. She walked over and ran her hands over the smooth lines of the wood. It was beautiful. She didn't see any store tags like the ones visible on some of the other pieces in the room. As she examined it more closely, she started to suspect that it might be handmade. By Xander?

She recalled how he'd been absent a lot lately. He was always going here or there. Could this have been what had him so preoccupied? Was he creating all of this for their baby?

The impact of his actions caused an emotional lump to swell in her throat. Tears stung the back of her eyes. If the baby meant this much to him, why had he left? Why did he leave so much unsaid between them?

As the questions crowded into her mind, she moved out of the nursery, pulling the door closed behind her. Staying here wasn't going to help her. She needed to get away.

Lea went to her room, a room where they'd made love so recently. Memories of Xander were everywhere. She had to get away.

She pulled a duffel bag from the back of her closet. She grabbed random articles of clothes from the closet and tossed them on the bed. Her movements were abrupt, causing her to almost trip over her own feet.

She couldn't get out of here fast enough. It felt like if she stayed here any longer the memories would suffocate her. That was it. Different scenery and some fresh air would hopefully give her a clear perspective. If she could get away from everything that reminded her of Xander, she'd be able to breathe easy. But she wondered if that place existed.

Knock. Knock.

Xander?

Lea's heart raced. Had he come back? What should she say to him? She had no answers.

"Lea?" The front door creaked open as Popi let herself inside.

Lea's heart slowed and she expelled a pent-up breath. "I'm back here."

It was good that her friend was here. It would save her a trip over to Popi's place. But how did she explain all of this to her?

When Popi appeared in her bedroom doorway, her gaze landed on the clothes scattered on the bed. "Going somewhere?"

"Yes."

"With Xander?" Popi glanced around as though searching for him.

"No. By myself. Xander is gone."

"Oh. Um… Do you want to talk?"

Lea shook her head. She didn't think she could speak of Xander without breaking down in tears and that was the last thing she wanted right now. If she could just get away from the place where she'd spent so much time with Xander, she'd be okay.

Without meeting her friend's gaze, she said, "I need you to handle things for a few days."

"But where are you going?"

Lea hadn't stopped to think about that. Her mind was in a tizzy. She could leave the island altogether and head for the mainland. There were plenty of places to lose herself there. But she wasn't up for sightseeing and she really didn't want to deal with people.

And then a thought came to her. When she'd first arrived on the island, she'd done a lot of exploring, even stumbling upon an abandoned cabin. In that moment, she knew where she could go. The secluded spot would give her a chance to formulate a plan. Because even though she'd spoken to her mother and they'd started the process of patching up their relationship, Lea realized this island and the people on it were now her home. There had to be a way to save it that she hadn't thought of yet—even if it came down to an internet fundraiser. She would not lose the island.

CHAPTER TWENTY

WHERE IS SHE?

It was late when Xander returned to the island. Still, he'd only been gone for not quite twelve hours. How far could she get?

He inwardly groaned when he thought of the answer. Lea could have gone quite far. He'd searched every room in the bungalow and her office. She was nowhere to be seen. And that was when he realized the one person who would know where to locate her—Popi. They were as close as two friends could be.

He knew it was late but that didn't stop him from approaching Popi's door. Surely she would understand the urgency. The longer he let this thing linger, the further Lea slipped away from him. The thought of losing Lea forever had him urgently knocking on the door.

When the door didn't immediately swing open, he started to worry that Popi wasn't home. But where else would she be on the island? It didn't exactly have a night life unless there was a wedding. And he knew from his work on the island that there was none scheduled for the evening.

He knocked again. "Popi! It's Xander. I need your help."

The door swung open. Popi stood there with her hair mussed up as she clutched a short white robe around her and glared at him. "What's going on?"

"I'm really sorry to disturb you this late." And he was sorry, but that didn't stop him. He had a feeling that if he didn't find Lea soon, she would plan a new life that didn't include him and he wouldn't have a chance to change her mind. "I need to find Lea. She's gone."

Popi sighed. "And this couldn't have waited until morning?"

He shook his head. "I messed up real bad. And now I need to find her. I need to tell her… I need to tell her so many things."

Popi studied him for a moment and then she shook her head. "I can't help you."

When she began to close the door, he stuck out his foot, blocking the door from closing the whole way. "Listen, I know I screwed up in more than one way. I shouldn't have left her. I should have stayed and fixed things. I made a mistake. Surely you can understand. You've made mistakes, haven't you?"

"Sure, I have. But walking away from someone that you're supposed to care about after you've screwed up royally, well that's a special kind of mistake. It's the kind of mistake that makes the other person need time to sort things out in their head."

"And that's why I have to get to her."

"Leave her be. You can speak to her when she gets back—"

"It'll be too late. She'll have written me out of her life and we all know how stubborn she can be when she feels as though someone she cares about has betrayed her."

"You mean her parents?"

He nodded. "I've been trying to talk her into reconciling with them, but she's hesitant. If she does the same thing with me, I don't know how I'll ever win her back." He pleaded with Popi with his eyes. "Please help me. I love Lea and she doesn't know it. It might make a difference in what she decides to do next."

Popi let go of the door and crossed her arms above her rounded abdomen. "I don't want to, but I believe you. But you have to understand that I made a promise to my best friend not to tell anyone where she went."

He was the one to sigh this time. "And you are worried that Lea will see this as a betrayal." He hated what he had to say next. "I can't ask you to do that, not only for your sake but also for Lea's. She needs you."

He turned to walk away. He'd just reached the stepping stones when he heard Popi call out to him. He paused and turned back.

"If you need a place to stay tonight, I know of a little secluded hut."

Was she trying to get him out of the way? Or was she trying to tell him something? He quietly waited for her to go on.

"With it being out of the way, it would be a good place for you to figure out your next step. If you're interested, I can tell you how to get there." A small smile pulled at Popi's lips.

And then he knew she was giving him directions to reach the love of his life. He agreed and she gave him the instructions. She told him he might want to wait for daybreak before heading into the rough terrain and getting lost. But he couldn't stand to live any longer with this rift between him and Lea. With every passing moment it felt like Lea was slipping away.

And so he set off down the path with a flashlight and a few supplies. He would find her and then he'd plead his case. He just prayed Lea would be willing to listen.

CHAPTER TWENTY-ONE

SLEEP ELUDED HER.

Lea stretched out on the small bed and stared into the darkness. She had never felt more alone, not even when she'd packed up and left everything that she knew and loved in Seattle. This loneliness was so much deeper and so much more painful.

But Xander had made his choice of what was most important to him when he'd left before explaining exactly what was going on with his sister. Now that she'd calmed down, she recalled a few of the words she'd overheard when she entered the bungalow while he video-chatted with his sister.

His sister had said that she was only doing what she thought was best for him. And he'd told her he didn't need her being so overprotective. He could take care of himself. It was shortly after that that he'd noticed Lea's presence.

At the time, Lea had been so upset and wallowing in the pain of betrayal that she hadn't bothered to consider what Xander might have meant. But out here, away from the drama, she could think more clearly. And she didn't like what she was thinking...

She loved Xander.

She missed Xander.

She flopped over in bed and fluffed her pillow. Thinking of Xander and missing him wasn't doing her any good. How was she supposed to get over him?

Just then she felt a kick. *The baby.* It caught her completely off guard. She rolled onto her back and placed her hand on her expanding abdomen, willing it to move again. Each day, the baby was getting stronger. Lea wished Xander was there to share this special moment with her.

What would have happened if she'd stayed at the bungalow and waited for him? Would he return? Would he wonder what had happened to her?

He'd never find her because she'd only told one person where she'd gone. And she'd sworn Popi to secrecy. Maybe that had been overkill, but she'd been running on pure emotions at the time.

She reached for her cell phone to text Popi but there was no signal out here. With a grunt, she returned the phone to the side table. Her hand pounded the pillow into what she hoped was a more comfortable position. And then she rested on her side and closed her eyes, willing sleep to take her to dreamland, where anything was possible, including happily-ever-afters.

Knock. Knock.

Lea's eyes sprang open. The beginning signs of dawn illuminated the room. Had she at last fallen asleep? She was pretty sure that was the case. But what had awoken her?

Knock. Knock.

"Lea?"

Was that Xander? It sure sounded like him.

She sat straight up in bed. It couldn't be Xander. He wouldn't even know where to find her. But someone was definitely pounding on her door.

She jumped out of bed and rushed to the door. She swung it open and stood there speechless when she saw a very tired Xander staring back at her.

"Can I come in?" he asked.

She pulled the door wide open and moved off to the side in order for him to enter. At last finding her voice, she asked, "What are you doing here?"

Even with heavy stubble covering his jaw and his hair mussed up, he looked so amazingly handsome. "I had to find you. I had to tell you I'm sorry."

"For leaving?" She was about to tell him that she understood, but he didn't give her the chance.

"For that. And for not realizing soon enough how important you are to me. And for my sister pulling that overprotective routine and coming here to investigate you after I told her we were going to become a family." He glanced down at the floor. "I guess I got ahead of myself when I told her that last part."

"Why didn't you tell me right away about your sister?"

He'd meant to and he had legitimate reasons why he put it off, but it boiled down to… "I couldn't at first. There was that accident with Joseph and Popi asked me to help fill in. And then I kept putting it off because I knew it would spell trouble for us and we were in such a good place."

"And you were afraid I'd think you betrayed me like my parents?"

He nodded.

"What my parents never understood and what I hope you'll understand is that I don't need anyone to protect me. I need a partner who is honest with me about everything—the good and the bad."

"I can do that." His eyes reflected the truth of his words.

Lea's heart swelled with hope. This was the second chance that she'd been lying in bed all night hoping for. She couldn't mess it up. "As for being a family, is that what you still want?"

His gaze met hers. "More than anything else. I know I've messed things up more than once, but I'd like a chance to make them right."

Her heart raced. He was saying all the right things. But there was just one more thing she needed to hear. "And if you could make them right, what would you say?"

His gaze searched hers. "I would say I'm sorry

I hurt you. I will do my utmost best to never do that again. And I'm sorry that I put my business ahead of our relationship. That will never happen again." When she sent him a doubtful look, he added, "I've just recently opened my eyes to the fact that I have a very capable number two. He is now on his way to Italy to handle this latest crisis."

"Really? I mean, you said it was so important. I don't want you to risk your company—"

"What I was risking was far more important than business." He reached out and took her hands in his own. "Lea, I love you. And I want to spend the rest of my life showing you just how much you mean to me."

Tears of joy spilled onto her cheeks. "I love you, too. I was just too stubborn to admit it to myself. But my mother helped me to see that I was closing myself off because I was afraid of being hurt again."

"Your mother? You spoke to her?"

Lea nodded as she squeezed his hands. And then she explained about her mother's phone dying while they were on a cruise. "And so I have you to thank for talking sense into me and welcoming my parents back into my life."

"Did you tell them about the baby?"

"I did. And I think my mother cried. Happy tears. They're even planning to fly here, which I know is a big thing for them as they were banished from the island by my grandparents."

"Maybe this baby will help bring everyone back together. After all, it worked for us. You are the only woman in the world for me."

"And you are the only man for me."

"In that case, I have a proposition for you." He dropped to one knee. "I know you've turned me down before and rightly so. But a lot has changed since then. I've learned a lot. I love you, Lea, with all my heart. And I can't imagine my life without you in it. Will you do me the honor of being my bride?"

Happy tears clouded her eyes. "I would love to be your bride."

Just then the baby kicked again. Lea took Xander's hand and pressed it to her abdomen. And then there was another movement. This time Xander's face lit up when he felt the baby move.

"He or she likes the idea." When Lea looked at her future husband, she saw that he was a bit misty-eyed, too.

Her heart overflowed with love. The future looked so amazing. There was nothing they couldn't accomplish—together.

EPILOGUE

Infinity Island, two weeks later...

"WE'RE GETTING MARRIED."

Lea was so happy she felt as though she was going to burst. First, Xander had told her that he loved her and then he'd swept her off on a trip to Seattle. He thought the peace she'd made with her parents deserved to be followed up with an in-person visit.

The trip had been amazing. Xander had been amazing. And then he had done something most unexpected: he'd asked her parents for their approval for him to marry their daughter. It might have been done a bit backwards, but it still touched Lea's heart.

And then atop the Sky Needle, with the sun setting and casting the most glorious streaks of pinks and purples through the sky, Xander had once again got down on one knee. This time he had the biggest, most sparkling diamond ring ever.

Lea remembered how everyone around them had grown quiet. You could have heard a pin drop if it hadn't been for the loud banging of her heart. It had echoed in her ears. But above it, she had heard Xander claim his love for her.

And now that they were back on Infinity Island, she couldn't be happier. "He proposed again." Lea held out her hand for Popi to see her sparkly engagement ring. "We're really and truly going to be a family."

"It's beautiful." Popi rushed forward and gave them both a big hug. She pulled back, looking at both of them. "I always knew this was going to work out. You both deserve your happily-ever-after."

"There's more." Lea wasn't sure how Popi was going to take the other news. "Our wedding is going to be the last wedding on the island."

In a blink, Popi's expression changed from one of excitement to one of horror. "You're shutting down the island? You're giving up?"

Lea felt bad for not phrasing it better. In her excitement, she'd just let the words tumble out. But she knew this island meant almost as much to Popi as it did to her. Infinity Island was home for them. "No, I'm sorry. I didn't mean to worry you." Lea turned to Xander. "Do you want to tell her?"

He shook his head. "You're doing fine."

Lea's heart fluttered in her chest as Xander gazed into her eyes. Every time he looked at her that way, her heart swelled with love. She wondered if it would always be that way—even fifty years from now.

Lea turned back to her best friend. "The reason

ours will be the last wedding is that while we're off on an extended honeymoon, the island will be undergoing renovations."

Popi's face lit up and then she clapped her hands in delight. "That's wonderful. This place could really use some help. If there's anything I can do, just let me know."

Lea's gaze dipped to her friend's expanding midsection. "I think you'll have enough to do with your little niece or nephew on the way. Your sister and brother-in-law must be so excited."

"They are. We all are." Popi's gaze lowered. "You know, in the beginning I wasn't so sure about this whole plan."

"You certainly hid it well."

"I didn't want anything to ruin this for my sister. I kept telling myself that it was nerves."

"And how do you feel now?"

"Excited. I can't wait to see my sister with the baby in her arms."

"Even though you have to go through childbirth."

"That's the part I'm trying not to think about. But enough about me. Tell me more about the renovations."

"We're relocating Xander's executive offices to the island."

"Really?" Popi's gaze moved to Xander. "And

you're okay with this? Won't you feel a bit isolated out here?"

"Hey," Lea said, "are you trying to talk him out of this?"

"No." The smile slipped from Popi's face. "Never mind. I didn't mean anything by the questions."

"They're legitimate questions," Xander said. "And I'm happy to answer them. I would follow Lea wherever she led."

"You would?" Lea asked.

He turned to her. "I haven't gotten to this level of success without knowing a good thing when I see it. And so I'm not going to let you slip away. I need you in my life."

Lea moved to him and wrapped her arms around his neck. "You do say the sweetest things. And in case you didn't know, I need you, too."

His hands wrapped around her waist as she lifted up on her tiptoes to press her lips to his. Her lips had barely touched his when she heard Popi clearing her throat rather loudly. Heat rushed to Lea's cheeks. With great reluctance, she pulled away from Xander.

"Sorry." Lea couldn't believe how easy it was for this man to totally distract her. If this was love, she didn't ever want it to end.

"Not a problem." Popi grinned at her. "If I had a man as hot as him, I'd get distracted, too."

"You will," Lea said. "I bet he's just around the corner."

"Not with this baby on board. A man wouldn't even think of getting near me."

"You won't be pregnant much longer," Lea said encouragingly. "At least that's what I keep telling myself as each day my toes seem to get further and further away from me."

Popi laughed. "Just wait until your third trimester—they disappear from sight."

"Seriously," Lea said with a sigh, subduing the banter. "Will you be all right while the island is being renovated? Do you have someplace to go?"

Popi placed a protective hand over her rounded abdomen. "Now that you mention it, I was hoping to take some time off to visit with my sister and her husband. My sister wants to be with me for the birth. So this will work out perfectly."

"Wonderful." Lea smiled broadly. "We have so much to look forward to." And then she turned to the man of her dreams. "It doesn't get any better than this."

* * * * *

*Look out for the next story in the
Greek Island Brides trilogy*

Coming soon!

*If you enjoyed this story,
check out these other great reads
from Jennifer Faye*

Heiress's Royal Baby Bombshell
Miss White and the Seventh Heir
Beauty and Her Boss

All available now!